Falling Hard

Falling Hard

A FALLING FOR THE FREEMANS ROMANCE

KATE HEWITT

TULE
PUBLISHING

DEDICATION

To all my lovely readers who have followed me from story to story. You are the reason I do what I do.

Thank you!

CHAPTER ONE

"I THINK IT'S time to sell the hotel."

Quinn Freeman stiffened with both tension and shock as he gazed out at a wintry Central Park. Drifts of dirty snow were heaped alongside the cobbled pavements, and the leafless trees' stark branches were rimed with ice.

"Quinn?" His mother's voice was gentle and sad. "What do you think?"

"I suppose it's more important what Adam thinks," Quinn answered as he turned around to face his mother. "He's the one calling the shots." His older brother was CEO of Freeman Enterprises and never let his two younger brothers forget it. Certainly he hadn't let Quinn forget it when he'd tried to take part in the family business.

Margo sighed and shook her head. "It's an emotional decision for all of us."

"Yes, although not as much for me." The tightening of his gut and the sudden lurch of emotion belied his words, but Quinn continued, his voice smooth and toneless, "I don't even remember the hotel or our life there. We left when I was six."

"I know." His mother's mouth turned down at the corners and she looked away. Quinn's gut gave another painful twist. Of course his mother knew. The Freemans had left Creighton Falls over twenty years ago, after the death of Peter Freeman, beloved husband and father, in a drowning accident. An accident that had involved Quinn, even if he couldn't remember a single thing about it. Even if he wished every day of his life that it hadn't happened.

He sat across from his mother, patting her hand and wishing he knew what to say. The Freemans had stopped talking intimately years ago; everything just glided on the surface. He was amazed his mother had mentioned the hotel at all.

Margo smiled her thanks and then sat back in the silk-patterned wingback chair, her hands folded in her lap. "It's been a long time," she said softly.

Yes, it had. Maybe even long enough to forget, except he'd never remembered in the first place. "Why are you bringing this up now?" Quinn asked. Creighton Falls had been off-limits in family conversation for over two decades.

"It seemed a good time to discuss it with you, considering how rarely you're home." She lifted elegantly arced eyebrows. "When are you off again?"

"I'm not sure." He'd spent the last six months bartending on the beaches of Thailand, just another one of his many jaunts abroad, but at twenty-eight years old his nomadic lifestyle was definitely starting to pale. The trouble was, the only other thing he wanted to do was forbidden to him.

Margo Freeman pressed her lips together, her gaze turning distant. "The hotel is becoming derelict," she told him. "I've received a warning from the county council claiming it's a dangerous building, and they want it condemned."

"I thought we had someone taking care of the place." Quinn knew the Creighton Falls Hotel had been empty since they'd shut it twenty-two years ago, when they'd all abruptly pulled out of Creighton Falls and its hard memories. "A caretaker to keep things tidy."

"We did at first, but I'm afraid it's slipped over the years. I've never liked to think about Creighton Falls, and Adam is so busy..." Margo shrugged slender shoulders. "I'm ashamed that we've let it get in such a state. I suppose it was easier simply not to think about it."

"That's understandable."

"In any case, it was too much work for one man. The caretaker we hired had trouble enough keeping on top of it before he retired."

"And now?" Quinn asked.

"Something needs to be done."

"What does Adam say?"

"I haven't had a chance to talk to him yet." Margo tilted her head, her gaze resting thoughtfully on her youngest son. Quinn felt its gentle probing and shifted in his seat. His mother didn't usually inquire too deeply about his life or his choices, but she looked poised to dig a little now. "I thought perhaps you could go up and have a first look at the place. See how much work needs to be done to get into a decent shape for sale."

"Me?" Quinn stared at her in blatant surprise. In the seven years since he'd dropped out of university, his mother had hardly asked anything of him. No one had really ever, because he was the youngest son, the surprise baby, the kid on the fringes of the family, who just tagged along for the ride. He'd got used to things being that way; he almost liked it. "Why me?"

"Why not you?" Margo countered. "You know how busy Adam is and Jacob is in Bolivia. You're the natural choice."

"You mean the only choice." Adam was running the world and Jake was CEO of his own company, For Free World Disaster Recovery Services. He was more of a globetrotter than Quinn, but instead of mixing cocktails and pouring shots, he was saving lives and being a hero.

"Call it what you will, Quinn," Margo said, "but it would help me if you'd go up to Creighton Falls." Pain flashed across his mother's face and her mouth twisted. "You know I can't bear to be up there. Maybe it's weakness, but…"

"No, it's not." Remorse soured inside him, a corrosive acid that had already eaten away most of his soul. "Of course I'll go," he said gruffly. His mother didn't ask him for much, but when she finally did, Quinn knew he'd say yes. He could never make up for what happened when he was six, for being alive now when his father was dead. He'd do whatever he could to try, though.

Margo reached forward and touched her son's cheek with the tips of her fingers. "Thank you, Quinn," she said softly.

Quinn didn't reply.

"SOMEONE'S UP AT the hotel."

Meghan O'Reilly glanced up from where she was lying on her back, underneath a kitchen sink, without much interest. "Someone's always nosing up around there. The county council want to have the place condemned, and kids sneak in to smoke or drink or make out." She made a face as she gave the valve under Brenda Wickley's sink a twist with her wrench. "Or all three."

"I don't mean someone like that." Brenda swiped a strand of peroxide-blond hair from her eyes, an e-cigarette dangling from her lips, and squinted out her kitchen window that looked out on Creighton Falls' overgrown green. The tufty grass was patched with dirty snow; it was late February, and winter still held upstate New York in its fierce grip, even though everyone was hoping for spring.

"Who, then?" Meghan asked. She scooted out from underneath the sink and started putting her tools away. "That should do it, Brenda."

Brenda sucked hard on her e-cigarette. "You're a marvel, Meghan—"

"It was an easy job," Meghan said, dismissively. "You

could have done it yourself."

"If I knew one end of a wrench from the other," Brenda agreed. "Anyway, back to the hotel. Someone important is up there. Someone with a Beamer."

"A BMW?" Meghan's hands stilled on the toolbox. No one in Creighton Falls had that kind of fancy car. It was pointless in a place that required off-road capabilities for most of the year.

"Yes," Brenda said smugly. "A BMW. Who do you think that is?"

"Not a Freeman." It was the conclusion Brenda was obviously jumping to, but there hadn't been a Freeman in Creighton Falls in over twenty years, never mind that they'd once run the town.

"Who else could it be?" Brenda countered, tapping her e-cigarette on the edge of a plastic ashtray even though the thing generated no ash. "Sally Jackson is secretary to someone on the council, and she said they've been writing Margaret Freeman about the place. Saying something needs to be done before it falls down."

"Why should that make a difference?" Meghan answered. "The Freemans haven't bothered about the place for years, and they've never been back to Creighton Falls." A bitterness she'd thought she'd put to rest niggled her insides. So what if the Freemans had left? So had a lot of other people.

"Maybe they'll bother now."

"To do what? Reopen it again?" Meghan shook her head.

"Hardly."

"Sell it, maybe."

"If they can find a buyer for that ramshackle old place." Meghan loved Creighton Falls fiercely, had spent her whole life there, but there could be no denying that the closure of its one hotel had taken it off the tourists' map.

When she'd been little, Creighton Falls had been a tourist destination, admittedly an off-the-beaten-trail one, with a few quaint shops and a couple of restaurants. When she'd been little, her father had had a job as a tour guide for city types who wanted to fish on the St. Lawrence River. People had stayed in the hotel and shopped in the town and eaten in the restaurants.

Then the hotel had gone empty and the town had deteriorated, shops closing, people moving. Residents had tried to keep things going; Elsie McGuinness ran the diner, and Fiona had taken over an old carpet store on the edge of town and turned it into a bakery. Don Furman sold chainsaw sculpture at local craft fairs, and Sam Taylor offered ice fishing in the winter. People made do, jogging along as best as they could, but nothing could make up for the loss of the town's grand hotel.

"Well, I think it's interesting," Brenda said with a bit of a huff. "I don't know anyone who owns a Beamer."

"Me neither," Meghan answered. "But in any case, I doubt they're staying."

Brenda wagged a nicotine-stained finger at her. "You're

too cynical for someone your age, Meghan."

"My age?" Meghan smiled and raised her eyebrows. "I'm twenty-eight."

"Wait until you're fifty and you've seen something of the world. Then maybe—"

"I might not have ever left Creighton Falls," Meghan answered, and just kept herself from adding that neither had Brenda, "but I've seen plenty of human nature."

Brenda's face softened. "I know that, honey—"

Not wanting to endure Brenda's pity, Meghan shoved her arms into her parka and then grabbed her toolbox. "Okay, that's it, then. Let me know if you have any more problems with the sink."

"I will." Brenda's face brightened. "Are you going to the talent show on Friday night?"

"How on earth could I miss it?" The Creighton Falls Talent Show was a highlight of the town's social calendar. Plus there was pie. "I'll be there," she promised Brenda. *With earplugs*, she added silently. Billy Kargas's rendition of *I Will Always Love You* could strip paint from the walls, not that anyone would ever tell him so.

Outside, the air was cold and damp with not even a hint of spring to lift the spirits. The sky was a leaden gray, the snow, now several weeks since the last fall, nearly the same color. A thin layer of ice covered the puddles in the rutted road, and Meghan carefully stepped over one, knowing all too well how a boot could break through and she'd find herself shin-deep in icy, muddy water.

"Roll on, spring," she muttered, even though spring in upstate New York meant lots of mud. Still, it also meant fields full of flowers, the sun sparkling off the river, a hint of warmth in the air. She threw her toolbox in the back of her battered pickup and climbed into the driver's side, resting her hands lightly on the wheel as she took a moment simply to be. She'd been rushing from one job to another all day; the one benefit of being the area's only plumber was that she was rarely out of work, but sometimes she felt the toll of the relentless pace.

She checked her phone for messages from her younger sister, Polly, who worked in a supermarket near Watertown, and was relieved to see there were none. Some days she might get a dozen messages from her sister, most of them asking the most random questions or simply to tell her something she thought was interesting. Sometimes, though, the texts were important; Polly had gotten upset or misunderstood something, and Meghan had to keep her sister from melting down.

Meghan had long ago learned how to best manage Polly; she'd had to, when her mother had moved out to Arizona with her new husband, and her dad, although around, wasn't up for much in the parenting department.

She loved Polly with every cell of her being, would defend her to the death, but managing her day after day took its toll.

Meghan started the truck and pulled away from the curb, squinting as she glanced up toward the derelict hotel. The gold lettering on the sign out front was chipped and faded, and the iron scrollwork surrounding it was long gone. The hotel's windows were shuttered or broken; some of them were missing all of their glass panes, so they were nothing more than gaping holes, looking like empty eyesockets in a falling-down face. The decorative gingerbread that had graced the roofline was now rotting, much of it missing. The wide, sweeping porch that spanned the entire front of the building was bowed and clearly rotten.

Built as it was on the highest point of the green, it was meant to be the town's crowning glory. Instead it was the building equivalent of Miss Havisham's wedding dress.

Meghan drove slowly by the building, noticing the Beamer parked in the empty lot behind the hotel. She put on the brakes, her gaze sweeping over the place, but she couldn't see anyone moving about.

Had one of the Freeman brothers actually come back? And if the Freemans sold the hotel, what would it become? Maybe a hotel, but more likely it would be turned into something useful, a nursing home or subsidized housing. Meghan sighed and put her foot on the gas pedal. She had enough going on in her life without worrying about the hotel, or wonder for one minute about the faraway Freeman brothers.

CREIGHTON FALLS WAS a dump. Quinn stood outside his car, hands planted on hips, as he gazed at the scruffy green and the dilapidated gazebo that graced it. On the far side he could see a rusty slide and some broken swings half-covered in dirty snow.

The hotel was definitely a blight on the town's landscape, but it wasn't the only falling-down building here. Not by a long shot.

Admittedly, the town possessed some charm. The old Victorian houses still held the gracious elegance of an earlier age, with their cupolas and intricate gingerbread. And the scenery was spectacular—stands of towering pines and cedars, rolling hills, and of course the river.

Resolutely Quinn trained his gaze on that sparkling ribbon of water in the distance. It was beautiful, even if the sight of it made his stomach cramp. Since returning to Creighton Falls – he'd searched his brain for forgotten memories, hoping something about this dilapidated town would stir something in his head or heart about the first six years of his life. Nothing had.

He'd spent the afternoon walking through the downstairs of the hotel, noting the rotting floorboards, the wallpaper coming off in long, moldy strips. It had felt like walking through a ghost town or a haunted house, everything old and faded and rotten, and yet just *left*. The hotel's grand reception room still had most of its furniture, wingback chairs and marble end tables and velveteen sofas, all of it now moldy and reeking. He hadn't dared to go up the front stairs to the second floor; underneath the moldy carpet—someone had removed the brass stair rods—he suspected the floorboards were rotten and he'd plummet to his death if he took one wrong step.

In any case, he'd seen enough. The hotel was a disaster, and should be rightly condemned, and if his mother wanted a chance in hell of selling it, it was going to need a lot of work first.

A bitter wind blew from the river and Quinn shivered despite his down parka. A soft, purple dusk was already settling on the town, the green soon lost in shadows, a few stars twinkling in the indigo sky. It was a beautiful scene, with the lighted windows of the houses around the green lending it a cozy cheer that gave Quinn an unexpected pang.

Had he been happy here? Had he played on that green, run inside to a house that he no longer could identify? He could almost imagine it, but that's exactly what it was. Imagining. Nothing felt real or remembered.

He got in his car and drove past six pickup trucks parked alongside the green, wincing slightly at what a fish out of water he was. He'd traveled enough to think himself fairly worldly wise; he'd picked up a spattering of a half a dozen languages during his various bartending stints, but Creighton Falls was another matter entirely. He didn't belong here. Maybe he never had.

His fingers tightened on the wheel as his mind bumped

up against that dark, blank spot once more. Most people had memories of before they were six. Maybe not many, but surely a few. The first grade spelling bee. A birthday party. *Something.* Why the hell didn't he have any? Had that afternoon on the ice wiped his memory clean? It was as if a curtain had come down in his mind, in his heart, and even now he wasn't sure he wanted to lift it. Because maybe his mind chose not to remember for a reason. Maybe if he remembered his father, he'd miss him more.

He drove out of Creighton Falls without looking back, and headed for Watertown twenty miles away. He'd booked into one of the town's budget hotels for the night and tomorrow he'd head back to the city and inform his mother that the place was a disaster.

Of course his mother was going to want a bit more information than that. She'd want a detailed list of what needed repairing and how much it would cost. She'd want to be able to give such a list to Adam. And making such a list would take weeks.

The thought of spending that much time in Creighton Falls made Quinn uneasy. He'd had a prickling between his shoulder blades the whole time he'd been walking around that hotel, as if his subconscious had sensed someone was watching and waiting, ready to creep up on him. Stupid, maybe, to be unnerved by an empty hotel, but he couldn't quite shake the feeling.

As he drove through Watertown, he noted the beautiful

buildings in the town's faded downtown area, a town hall, an old church, with most of the stately Victorian buildings now given over to discount chains and charity stores. Quinn parked at his hotel and checked in before deciding to hit the town's streets in search of a meal and a drink.

Quinn found a bar near the town hall, a pokey little dive with fake wood paneling and booths of ripped red vinyl. Still, it offered hamburgers along with alcohol and that's what Quinn wanted.

He slid onto a stool at the Formica-topped bar and ordered a burger and a whiskey. A few trucker-types with baseball caps pulled low over their faces were hunched over their beers, and from the corner of his eye Quinn saw that the only other people in the place were a gaggle of twenty-something women in stretchy tops and short skirts. He could see they were eyeing him openly, and he deliberately looked away and took a sip of his drink. No need for female company tonight, even though he wasn't normally averse. Tonight he felt too edgy and restless, those non-memories stirring up things inside him that had lain stagnant for a long time.

"Hey there, stranger."

Quinn turned to see a young woman from the table in the corner standing in front of him. A quick onceover told him she would be pretty, if she'd held back a little on the face paint and cheap, tight clothing. She'd planted one hand on her hip and stuck her leg out, a parody of a pose, the smile on her face so forced and fake Quinn inwardly cringed.

"Hi," he said neutrally, and looked away again. He didn't want to be rude, but this woman clearly needed no encouragement. He saw her glance back at her friends who were clearly egging her on. Then she slid onto the stool next to him.

"Buy me a drink?" she suggested and Quinn gritted his teeth.

"Sorry, I'm just about to leave." Her face fell in childish disappointment and he noted how round her cheeks were, how wide her eyes. Hell, she was little more than a kid. "Maybe next time," he said, simply to soften the blow, and too late he realized he shouldn't have said anything because she took it as encouragement.

"Why not now?" she answered, a pouty note entering her voice.

"I'm sorry, but I told you I'm leaving." He downed the rest of his whiskey and was about to get up when the girl, quite suddenly, plopped herself in his lap. Quinn had no choice but to put his hands on her waist, to keep her from sliding straight onto the floor. She threw her arms about his neck and he eased backward to keep her from planting a big one right on his lips.

Hell.

"Easy there," he said, trying for a smile because even now he had the bizarre impulse not to hurt her feelings. She seemed so *young.*

"I knew you were nice," she replied, and laid her head

15

against his shoulder, curling into him like a little kitten.

Quinn had no idea what to do. He'd had plenty of experience with women of all types, but nothing like this.

He glanced back at the girls in the booth, but they were all tittering behind their hands. The farmers hunched along the bar were looking avidly in the other direction.

"Listen…" he began, but before he could say anything else someone was throwing open the door of the bar so hard it banged against the wall, and then a woman was striding towards him, all glittering-eyed fury and swirling dark hair.

"Hey you," she snarled. "Get the hell away from my sister."

CHAPTER TWO

MEGHAN PLANTED HER hands on her hips, glaring at the man who was cradling Polly way too close. Her chest heaved and she tasted bile in her throat. She was furious, but she was also afraid. Anything could have happened to Polly. *Anything.*

"Look, I wasn't…"

"Do you know how old she is?" she demanded, even though the question wasn't really relevant. Polly was twenty-four, even if she didn't act like it. Even if she would never actually be an adult.

The man's face paled but he didn't release Polly, who had wrapped herself around him and was smiling up at Meghan as if they were all having a grand old time.

"Meghan," she chirruped. "I've made a new friend."

Meghan gritted her teeth, torn between rage and tears. *Oh Polly*, she wanted to cry. *If you only knew.*

"I think you have the wrong idea about what's going on here," he said quietly, but she heard an edge of anger in his voice that made her more furious.

"You think so, huh? I come in here and see you pawing

my sister, your hands everywhere…"

"Meghan, don't shout," Polly said.

"Let go of her," Meghan commanded, and the man tried to extract himself from Polly's winding grip.

"Gladly," he muttered. Two spots of color had appeared on each chiseled cheekbone, but the skin around his mouth was white. Meghan had the jolting sensation that this stranger was just as pissed off as she was. He was a good-looking stranger, that was for sure. Dirty blond hair streaked with both lighter blond and brown and hazel eyes. Chiseled cheekbones and a body to match. Polly had picked well—or not, depending on how you looked at it.

The man was trying to put Polly on the ground, but her sister was resisting. When Polly got something into her head, she didn't let go of it easily. Meghan felt a flicker of uncertainty, a cringing of shame. Maybe this man hadn't actually targeted her sister. Knowing Polly, her sister had targeted *him.* And then she'd gone and jumped to all sorts of conclusions.

"I like him," Polly said, confirming Meghan's suspicions, and she closed her eyes briefly, sent a prayer heavenward, asking for strength.

Meghan snapped her eyes open and saw the stranger staring at her, a frown settled between his brows. She felt something flip inside her at that narrowed look, and she turned to give her sister a careful smile. "I see that, Poll, but you don't know him. You remember what I said about strangers?"

Polly pouted but her grip had loosened enough for the man to finally fully extract himself and stand up. He flung a twenty-dollar bill onto the bar, sending a pointed glare toward the hunched backs of a couple of barflies who clearly hadn't wanted to get involved in an out-of-towner's dispute.

"Nice knowing you," the man muttered, and started walking towards the door. Polly let out a whine of dismay and Meghan grabbed her sister's arm.

"Come on, Polly. Let's go." The man disappeared out into the night, and Meghan considered going after him to apologize. But she couldn't deal with Polly and some stranger, and so she chose her sister.

"How did you know I was here?" Polly asked as Meghan marched toward the door.

"Your supervisor texted me and told me you were going out with some friends." Which had sent the alarm bells inside her head pealing.

"I was just having fun," Polly protested. "And that man was so nice. Tami said I should say hi to him."

Meghan stopped in front of the door, her whole body tensing. "Oh, Tami did, did she?" No doubt she thought it would be funny to watch Polly make a fool of herself. No doubt the girls fell over themselves laughing when they dolled Polly up in this ho-bag get-up.

Fury beating in her blood, Meghan arrowed a glare at the gaggle of girls in the corner, who giggled nervously in response. "You should know better," she told them in a hard voice. "Shame on you."

One girl, probably Tami, ducked her head. "We wouldn't have let anything bad happen to her. We just wanted to see…"

Rage spiked through Meghan, making it difficult to speak. "She's not your *plaything*," she finally ground out. "She's not your social experiment. She's a person, just like you, like anyone, who deserves respect and kindness and—and *decency*." The girls all hung their heads, avoiding meeting her eyes, and choking down her anger, Meghan stomped outside, bringing Polly with her.

"You weren't very nice, Meghan," Polly said in a small voice.

The wind funneling down Watertown's main street was bitter, bringing tears to Meghan's eyes. "Those girls weren't very nice, Polly," she said, although she knew her sister wouldn't understand.

Polly's lip wobbled. "But they're my friends."

"Some friends," Meghan muttered before she could keep herself from it, and Polly yanked her hand from hers.

"Don't say that!" she shouted. "You shouldn't talk that way about my friends." She wrapped her arms around herself, rocking back and forth.

"Oh, Poll." Meghan bit her lip, willing her own anger back. "I'm sorry. They are your friends, and I shouldn't say that about them. But…" She took a deep breath, trying to navigate these treacherous waters while having no idea how deep they could get. "Sometimes friends make mistakes. They don't do nice things. That's all." And she'd call Polly's supervisor tomorrow, make sure this didn't happen again. Polly loved her job bagging groceries, and Meghan didn't want her sister to lose her independence. But she could have got into a whole lot of trouble tonight. Just the thought of it made Meghan's stomach clench.

Meghan pulled her sister into a quick, wordless hug. "I love you, Polly," she whispered, and Polly clung to her.

"I'm sorry, Meghan."

Meghan knew Polly probably didn't understand what to be sorry for, but she appreciated the sentiment all the same. "Let's go home," she said. "When we get back I'll make you a cheese and pickle sandwich."

"And a Coke?" Polly asked, her eyes brightening, her expression alert and hopeful.

"And a Coke," Meghan promised. Her sister had the same thing for dinner every single night, without exception.

"Okay."

Meghan shepherded Polly toward the truck, breathing a sigh of relief when she finally had her sister safely buckled.

A drizzly, needling sleet was starting to fall as Meghan pulled away from the curb. As she headed for the highway, she saw a man walking down the sidewalk, shoulders hunched and head tucked low against the sleet. It was the man from the bar, with his fancy puffa parka and top-of-the-line hiking boots. Meghan started to slow down so she could apologize for yelling at him, but then she realized he could have done anything to Polly; maybe he just hadn't gotten the chance. Her mouth in a firm line, she kept driving.

QUINN WOKE UP with the fading wisps of a dream drifting like smoke through his mind. He'd been back in the hotel, but not as it was, dirty and derelict, but as it once had been. Pure white snow had been piled like cotton candy outside the windows that were framed with sumptuous crimson velvet drapes. A huge Christmas tree twinkling with a million colored lights graced the large drawing room, by a roaring fire.

But beyond those physical details, the dream held something more: poignant, deeply felt emotion, a sense of childhood wonder and profound joy. He lay there, the weak, wintry sun filtering through his hotel room's mustard-yellow curtains, blinking in the early morning gloom and trying to hold onto that elusive feeling. He couldn't ever remember feeling that way. That *happy*.

The dream was already receding like a dawn mist, retreating to the foggy corners of his mind as he came more fully awake. More recent memories took place of those distant, half-forgotten ones—the bar last night, the young woman plopping herself in his lap, and her sister storming into the bar, everything about her blazing.

That woman had been a far more appealing proposition

than the one he'd had in his lap. Long, wavy dark hair, bright blue eyes, and a curvy, athletic figure, or so he suspected underneath the parka and jeans.

Not, of course, that Quinn had any intention of complicating his stay in Creighton Falls with a fling or anything like it. Besides, he'd never see her again. Thankfully.

The dream was well and truly forgotten now, and that sense of wonder he'd held onto for a few precious seconds had dissipated, leaving him flat.

He needed to go back to Creighton Falls, go through the hotel again. Bring in professionals to assess what the major repair work would be before they could put it on the market. Then he could get back to the business of living instead of wandering through the forgotten town as if he were a ghost. Sighing, Quinn rolled out of bed.

Thirty minutes later he'd had a cup of black coffee and a couple of fried eggs in the hotel's restaurant and was heading north on Highway 81, the road bordered by trees on either side, falling away to farm fields patched with snow as he took the exit for Creighton Falls.

He drove slowly into the town, taking a little more time to examine the buildings than he had before, from the faded beauty of the Victorian houses on the outskirts to the shuttered storefronts by the green, the junky play equipment half-hidden by the snow, the peeling paint on the gazebo. He could see the bones of something beautiful in this town, hidden beneath dirty snow and rotting wood. He could imagine it as it might have been, a dozen or a hundred years ago, freshly painted and bustling with life.

None of it stirred any memory in him, though, and after parking the car in the lot behind the hotel, he paused for a moment, taking in the town, breathing in the cold, fresh air, and wondering if he really had lived here once, and whether the Christmas tree in his dream had been fantasy or memory.

In the distance, behind the row of storefronts, Quinn saw the glint of sun on ice, and knew it was the St. Lawrence River. He averted his eyes, felt an uncomfortable tightening in his chest. He'd avoid the river.

Someone came out of the diner across the green, an elderly man in a red plaid coat and baggy overalls. He paused in front of the door, squinting toward Quinn, and then he ambled down the street. Quinn went into the hotel.

The damp, musty air smelled just as old and unlived in as he remembered, and the hotel didn't look any better in the bright morning sun than it had in yesterday afternoon's oncoming twilight. It needed, Quinn reflected, a *lot* of work. Maybe more than he even realized. Peel back the rotting floorboards, strip the peeling wallpaper, and he might find something worse and more expensive to fix. But there was only one way to find out.

He went through the downstairs of the hotel again, more slowly this time, making notes on everything he noticed. They'd have to get rid of most of the furniture, strip the walls and repair the floors. He flipped a few switches but the electricity had been turned off long ago. He did find the valve for the water in a room in back of the kitchen and turned it on. Checked the sink and after a few seconds, when pipes clanked and creaked in protest, a few rusty drops of water dribbled out of the faucet. He turned it off again and headed outside.

The morning's clouds had been burned off by a wintry sun that gilded everything in gold. The air felt clean and fresh and with a sense of purpose buoying his step, Quinn went in search of the town's library, and some reliable Internet access.

He'd seen the sign for the library pointing down the green, the opposite direction from the highway. He walked past a couple of houses, a quaint, shuttered ice cream parlor that looked to be open only in the summer months, and a sign for a boat launch that pointed down a dirt road to the river. Then he found the library, a one-story, shingled building that was open only two days a week, and today was fortunately one of them. Quinn headed inside.

The librarian, a granny type who looked avidly curious to see a stranger strolling into her domain, immediately asked if she could help.

Quinn glanced around the tiny room, noting the shelf of well-thumbed paperback romances, a new fiction section which included all of four books, and a couple of battered armchairs where a few elderly people were reading the newspapers, rustling the pages ostentatiously as he spoke to the woman at the desk.

"Do you have a computer?"

"Oh, yes. We have *two*," she said proudly, and Quinn suppressed a smile. There was something strangely endearing about this shabby town.

The woman helped him to log onto the Internet which moved at a creaking pace—broadband hadn't come to this part of the state yet—and Quinn typed in the search engine for building contractors in the area.

Five minutes later, the page of results loaded, and within another half hour he'd managed to get names and numbers. He thanked the woman for her time and she leaned forward, clearly overcome by curiosity.

"You're a Freeman, aren't you, dear?"

Quinn tensed in surprise before he found a smile. "As a matter of fact, I am."

The woman nodded, clearly pleased to have her suspicions confirmed. "So which one are you? You don't look old enough to be Adam…"

It was unsettling to have this stranger so familiar with his family. "I'm Quinn."

"The baby. *Oh…*" She put one hand to her mouth, her eyes wide and dark with sympathy, and Quinn had to keep himself from recoiling. Did everyone in this town know him, his history? Seemed they did.

"Anyway." His smile was getting harder to keep on his face and his cheeks ached. "Nice to meet you," he said, even though they hadn't actually met, and he strode out of the library.

He walked back to the hotel, and when his phone finally registered reception by the town green he made a couple of calls. He left a message for the local plumber, arranged for an electrician to come out, and then called a building contractor, who sounded as curious as the librarian.

"You thinking of renovating that old place?"

"Just getting it ready for sale," Quinn answered, and heard an audible sigh of disappointment.

"Shame. It was so beautiful once. But you'll remember, of course."

"Actually, I don't," Quinn answered pleasantly. "See you tomorrow."

He disconnected the call and shoved his phone into his pocket, staring at the empty green. On its far side a few customers were in the diner, which seemed to be the one place of activity in Creighton Falls' minuscule downtown. Maybe he'd have dinner there tonight. On second thought, he decided he preferred the relative anonymity of Watertown. He didn't think he could stomach more people shooting him curious glances, asking him who he was, remembering when he couldn't.

Quinn headed back to the hotel for another look, grimacing as the close air hit him in the face. What the hell was he doing here? He should head back to Watertown now, spend the afternoon in the comparative comfort of his hotel room, and then show up here when the contractor came back. Why torture himself by staying in the place any longer than necessary?

Quinn didn't know the answer to that question, wasn't sure if he wanted to. Something about this old place drew him, made him want to walk its rooms in search of what—? Memories? Answers? A way to explain the lapse in himself, make him understand the two decades since then? Some part of him wanted Creighton Falls to hold answers to questions he hadn't even realized he'd needed to ask.

Why can't I remember? What actually happened out there on the ice? Were we a happy family once, a normal family?

Did he really want to know the answers to those questions? He stood in the front hall, trying to imagine what it would have looked like twenty-two years ago, bustling with guests and staff. He ran a hand along the length of the stair banister, only to have it come away covered with slimy dirt.

Swearing under his breath, he went to the sink in the kitchen and turned the water on, waiting for the rust-colored water to run clear. He'd just put his slimed hands under the freezing water when a snapping sound came from somewhere below him, and the next thing Quinn knew a waterfall was cascading around his ankles.

"Damn it." He turned the taps off, but the water kept coming from below. Quinn wrenched open the cabinet under the sink, and saw a pipe leaking like a geyser. He hurried back to where he'd found the water valve, but the damned thing was stuck, and he was afraid of twisting it too hard and breaking the whole thing off. He knew this was just the first of many problems the hotel would offer him, but his inability to deal with it infuriated him. He hated feeling useless, unneeded. It was what had driven him away from home, kept him traveling the world. And now with every second he tried to figure out what to do, the room became even more flooded.

He yanked his cell from his back pocket and scrolled down for the plumber's number. Thankfully someone answered this time.

"O'Reilly Plumbing," a woman's voice answered on the second ring, her voice brisk and business-like.

"I need an emergency call out immediately," Quinn said. "A pipe has bust and the valve to turn it off is stuck fast."

"Where are you?"

"The Creighton Falls Hotel."

There was a tiny pause, and then the woman answered, "I'll be there in five minutes."

True to her word, a pickup truck pulled up next to Quinn's BMW just under five minutes later, as twilight was beginning to fall over the green. A woman climbed out of the cab. Quinn waited by the kitchen door; the room was now ankle-deep in rust-colored water.

The woman grabbed a toolbox from the back of her truck and strode towards him. It wasn't until she'd stepped into the kitchen light that Quinn actually made out her face, and realized who it was. The gorgeous and furious woman from the bar last night.

CHAPTER THREE

IT WAS THE man from the bar. Meghan recognized him instantly, from his dirty blond hair and chiseled jaw to his expensive hiking boots, now soaked in dirty water.

"You'd better let me through," she said, and shouldered past him, breathing in the scent of aftershave and good old male sweat before the rank smell of the hotel hit her. "Good Lord."

"It needs some work."

"You can say that again."

"The valve is in the back room, behind the kitchen."

She grabbed a wrench from her toolbox, found the valve, and turned the valve off; it took a little elbow grease, but she managed it. The man stood behind her, looking both relieved and annoyed that she'd solved the problem so quickly. Typical.

"I'd better look at the leak." She sidled past him, her tool belt bumping against his hip, before he thought to move out of the way.

She had a quick look at the leaky pipe, which was under the sink. No doubt the pressure of the water being turned on after decades of nothing in its pipes had been too much for the old system. "I can do a temporary patch on the pipe for now, but the whole thing will need replacing at some point. It's rusted right through."

She glanced at the mini-lake that had formed on the kitchen floor. "Do you have a mop?"

"Somewhere maybe." The man was staring at the water-logged kitchen with a mixture of irritation and despair. Meghan felt a stirring of pity for him. The room really was a mess. Hell, the whole place was a mess. The question was, what was he going to do about it? She didn't know which one he was, but he had to be a Freeman. He wore the mantle of privilege and money carelessly and acted as if he owned the place, which he probably did.

"You want some help?" she asked. He glanced up at her, wry humor lighting his eyes, making them look more golden than green.

"Now that's a change."

Meghan knew he was referring to her hissy fit in the bar. "About last night. I'm sorry."

"Did your sister explain?"

"Not exactly." He frowned, and Meghan braced herself for the inevitable question. *Is something... wrong with her?* She'd heard a version of that question over and over again in the last twenty years. The trouble was, no doctor or psychologist had ever come up with a good answer. Quinn, however, didn't say anything more about Polly.

"I could use the help, if you're offering," he said after a pause. "Thank you."

"It's all part of the service. I can't put a patch on the pipe until the floor is clear." She smiled, raising her eyebrows. "You do know you're paying me two hundred bucks for an emergency call out?"

"Extortionate," he said, but he was smiling. He stuck out a hand. "Quinn Freeman."

So he *was* a Freeman. She shook his hand, surprised at the ruggedness of his callused palm. "Meghan O'Reilly."

"Of O'Reilly Plumbing."

"That's it."

He nodded slowly, still not letting go of her hand. Meghan had to pull it back, and ignore the tingling sensation low in her belly. So he was good-looking. Big deal. "So," she said. "First we should find a mop."

Quinn found a couple of mops and an old bucket in one of the storerooms off the kitchen. They worked in tandem, pushing the excess water out the back door, leaving long, rusty streaks on the old linoleum. They didn't talk much as they worked, but half an hour later the room was cleaner than it was, which wasn't actually saying all that much, but still.

Meghan propped her mop against the wall and swiped a strand of hair from her eyes. Polly would be back from her job in Watertown soon, and Meghan was always there when her sister got home. She didn't want today to be any different. "This shouldn't take long," she told him as she rummaged in her toolbox for her rubber gloves, a metal file, and some epoxy compound. "But you should know that a leak usually signifies a bigger problem with the plumbing system."

Quinn rolled his eyes good-naturedly. "Yeah, I think there might be a bigger problem here."

She smiled, reluctantly charmed by him. She could tell he knew he was cute, and she thought that he probably surfed on his charm. Maybe all the Freemans did. "Okay, this won't take long." She scooted under the sink, conscious that she was sprawled out on the kitchen floor, which was strange because half of her job was sprawling on someone's floor. Still, she could feel Quinn's eyes on her, and she tugged her green work shirt down lower over her jeans.

She roughened the pipe with the file and then softened the epoxy compound between her hands before squashing it onto the leak. She reached into her toolbox for a tourniquet and wrapped it around the pipe.

"It should cure in about twenty minutes," she told Quinn as she stood up and took off the rubber gloves with a snap. "I'll take off the tourniquet and then you'll be good. For a while, anyway."

"You want something to drink while you're waiting?" Quinn asked, laughter lurking in his eyes, inviting her to join in. "I've got plenty of water."

Meghan laughed and shook her head. "No thanks."

"I've also got a couple of Cokes."

"That I'll accept," she said, and watched in admiration of his long, lean form as he turned and fetched a couple of cans from the counter. He handed one to Meghan and then popped his own, taking a long swallow that drew Meghan's attention to the strong column of his throat.

She focused on her own drink. "I'll need to get back as soon as this is dry," she said after taking a sip, and Quinn nodded. "I've got to be back home for my sister."

A question flickered in his eyes. "You live with her?" he asked, and Meghan had the sense that that hadn't been the one he was going to ask.

"Yes. She's... she needs me."

He nodded slowly, and Meghan felt a flicker of surprised gratitude that he didn't press, simply accepted the situation for what it was.

"Anyway," she said. "You should have someone come and look through all the plumbing, see if there are any more problem areas."

"I left a message asking you to do that this morning."

"You did?" She hadn't had time to check her messages yet.

His smile was a slow burn. "You're the only plumber in the area, aren't you?"

She nodded jerkily, discomfited by the effect of that smile. "For twenty miles."

"Then you'd better do the estimate. Can you come back

tomorrow?"

"Maybe…" Quinn Freeman was a handsome, charismatic man, even if they'd started badly back at the bar. He felt dangerous, at least to her. Far too much temptation for a small town girl whose only companions were blue-collar guys, most of them with beer bellies and baseball caps. But then she thought about the money. And spending a little more time with a man who made her pulse skip. "Okay." She paused, and then, because she couldn't keep herself from it, she asked the question that had to be on everyone's tongue. "Are you fixing up the hotel?"

"Yes, to sell." Quinn's expression had turned neutral, his voice even and toneless.

"Oh." She was surprised at how deflated she felt. "I guess it was coming sometime."

"You're not the first person who's sounded disappointed it's the case."

"Everyone in Creighton Falls would like to see the hotel restored." She nodded towards the front of the house and the bay windows that overlooked the green. "It would help the whole town to have the hotel back in business."

Quinn's mouth compressed. "You really think a single hotel is going to help this town?"

Meghan lifted her chin, her gaze clashing with his, a challenge stirring up her soul. "It's not that bad. And before the hotel closed, Creighton Falls had a lot more business. A craft store, a card place… it might not seem like much to you, but it was."

"I get that."

"Do you?"

Quinn sighed and raked a hand through his hair, the strands flopping back onto his forehead. He had white-blond streaks amidst the lighter brown, and Meghan wondered if he had his hair highlighted. He was probably the type. Manicures maybe, too. She glanced at his hands and saw that wasn't the case. Okay, so maybe she was being a little unfair.

They held each other's gazes for a long, taut moment. Damned if she would look away first.

Quinn sighed and glanced away. It didn't feel like a victory. "Well, you all should be happy we're going to sell it. Maybe someone else will turn it into a hotel."

"Not likely."

His hazel eyes, bright with irritation, blazed at her. "And yet you blame us for not keeping on with it?"

"The town was thriving when you were here," Meghan retorted, and heard the throb of emotion in her voice. "The hotel brought in a lot of tourism, with a lot of support services. A lot of jobs. It all went when you closed it." She swallowed hard, discomfited and embarrassed by how emotional she was being. She'd put the past to rest a long time ago. Or so she'd thought.

"I'm sure that's true," Quinn said, and his voice held a deliberately even tone that suggested latent anger. "But surely you realize there was a very good reason we left the way we did."

Because his father had died. Inwardly Meghan cringed. Yeah, she probably should have been a little more sensitive about that. "Sorry," she said meekly. "I know it must have been very difficult for all of you."

Quinn nodded tersely. "Yes, well. I don't actually remember any of it. I was only six."

"The same age as me."

"Oh?" He looked surprised, as if the thought that they'd once inhabited the same world—sort of—was unlikely. Which, considering their respective positions now, it was. "Then I guess you know how little you remember from that age."

"Actually I have a lot of memories from that age." Memories of being on her father's boat, the sun on her face, watching it play on the water. Memories of when things had been different. They'd been *good*.

Quinn's expression had become bland, even aloof, and he turned away from her. "Must be nice."

"Why are you selling the place now?" Meghan knew she should let it go, but somehow she couldn't. She hadn't realized how much of a nerve this issue touched. The loss of the hotel had been the end of her town, her father's career, her *family*.

"My mother thinks it's time." Quinn still didn't look at her. "The place is falling down. As you can see."

"You could have kept that from happening."

"Actually, I couldn't have." An edge had entered his voice again and he turned around to face her, his arms folded across his impressive chest. "My brother Adam, makes all the decisions for Freeman Enterprises."

Meghan stared at him in disbelief. "You don't have any say at all?"

"No." A muscle in Quinn's jaw bunched. "Adam never did like to share."

"But surely…"

"Trust me," Quinn snapped, "I don't. And it's not for want of trying. So just…" He jerked a shoulder in a shrug. "Leave it."

And so Meghan did. There was a lot about the Freeman family she didn't understand or even know. Clearly. "Do you still want me to come tomorrow?"

"You're the only plumber around, so yeah. I need that estimate. In the meantime," his flinty gaze rested on her, his expression implacable, "send me the bill."

QUINN LET OUT the breath he hadn't realized he'd been holding as Meghan O'Reilly walked out the kitchen door. He heard the slam of her truck's door and he swore under his breath. Meghan O'Reilly might have been sexy as hell, especially with a tool belt slung low on her slim hips, a sliver of golden flesh visible as she'd lain on the floor, fixing that damned pipe, but she'd also been pretty bitchy. Pretty pissed off, blaming him for every woe this town had ever encountered.

Quinn turned from the door, surveying the streaky floor and all the rest of the hotel's mess. Meghan had no right to blame him or his family for an entire town's descent into dilapidation. It couldn't have all been up to the hotel. Why hadn't someone from the town bought the damn building themselves? Of course, it had never been for sale.

Muttering another curse under his breath, he stalked from the room. The hotel's three large reception rooms, a lounge, a bar, and a dining room, seemed to mock him with their ruined wallpaper and forgotten furniture. He stood by the bay window, staring at the huge marble fireplace that had figured in his dreams. Tried to imagine it with a roaring fire, the flames casting dancing shadows across the Christmas tree that twinkled with colored lights, the room filled with light and laughter and love. All he saw was mold and dust.

And yet… Quinn couldn't tell if the sharp feeling under his breastbone was memory for something that once had been, or longing for something that never was. Either way it didn't feel good. He had a bizarre urge to kick or hit something, to *hurt*. All these memories and feelings that being here was raking up made him feel restless, edgy, like he didn't know who he was anymore. Where he belonged. He stared hard at the empty fireplace with its scattering of old ashes for another long moment, and then, abruptly, he turned away.

"So, WORD IS you were fixing a Freeman's leaky pipe."

Meghan let out a tired laugh as she fixed her cell phone between her ear and shoulder. "That almost sounds dirty, Hannah."

"*Was* it dirty?" Hannah teased. "Because word is this particular Freeman is rather delicious."

Meghan grimaced as she continued to load the dishwasher. "Who have you been talking to? Brenda?"

"Got it in one."

"Figures," Meghan said with a sigh. Brenda Wickley worked as a waitress at the town's one diner and was a notorious gossip. If Brenda knew about something, everybody did. Fast. "How did she even know—"

"Saw your truck in the hotel's parking lot."

"I've only been back from the job for half an hour—"

"Word travels fast in these parts."

"That sounds like a line from a bad Western." Meghan sank into a chair at the kitchen table, one eye on Polly, who was curled up on the sofa, watching TV in their living room.

"Seriously, give me the details. A Freeman is back in town?"

"Quinn Freeman, yes."

"Which one is he?"

"The youngest, I think." She didn't actually *know* the Freeman family. They might have run the town back in the day, but they hadn't rubbed elbows with the likes of her, not really.

"It's such a sad story, what happened to them," Hannah said quietly. Unlike her, Hannah hadn't grown up in Creighton Falls. She'd only moved there a year ago, when she'd started dating a local man, Sam Taylor. They'd gotten married at Christmas, and were now living as blissful newlyweds. Meghan would have been sickened by the sweetness if she didn't like them both so much.

"It is a sad story," she agreed. Like everyone else in Creighton Falls, she knew the basic facts of what happened. Peter Freeman had gone ice fishing with his sons, and had drowned trying to rescue his youngest son, who had fallen through the ice.

Quinn, Meghan realized with a little ripple of shock. How had she not realized that before? He must have been the one Peter Freeman had died trying to rescue. Who had lost his father in such a terrible way. She'd known that in an academic way, and yet the awful realization of it punched her in the stomach now.

And she'd been snipping at him for his family deserting the town. Could she be more of a shrew? Letting out a gusty sigh, Meghan closed her eyes.

"Meghan?" Hannah asked. "You okay there?"

"Yeah," Meghan answered heavily. "I just realized I need to apologize again to Quinn Freeman."

"*Again?* What, you two have some kind of history?" Hannah sounded like she hoped they had.

"Not at all," Meghan answered. "He just happens to

push some of my buttons."

"I like the sound of that."

"Now you're really sounding dirty. Honestly, Hannah, all I did was put a patch on a pipe. Standard job."

"So you won't see him again?"

"I'm going back tomorrow, to do an estimate on the rest of the building," Meghan admitted. "At least as much as I can. But it's just a job, I hope you realize. I don't need the town gossiping about me in any shape or form." Even if Quinn Freeman was certainly something to gossip about, in all sorts of ways.

She didn't normally go for pretty boys—not that she was going for Quinn Freeman. At all. And to be fair, she couldn't actually call him a pretty boy. His body was lean and hard, his hands callused from—well, something. And okay, yes, so she'd felt a flicker of physical attraction, but hell, who wouldn't? He was good-looking. Gorgeous, even, and she'd had very limited dating options in the last ten years. But she wouldn't and couldn't think about a Freeman that way. They lived in different worlds. And Quinn was only here to sell the hotel, and finally end a dream.

"So what is Quinn Freeman doing here, exactly?" Hannah asked. "Is he going to fix up the hotel?"

"Only enough to sell it," Meghan answered on a sigh. "Who knows what it will become?"

"Better something than nothing," Hannah replied philosophically. "That thing is a serious eyesore."

"I know." But she still felt disappointed. She didn't want that once grand hotel turned into a nursing home or corporate offices or affordable housing, although the likelihood was that it wouldn't be turned into anything. She doubted the Freemans would be able to find a buyer for a huge place like that. The house prices around there had gone through the floor years ago, and they hadn't come up much. But if they did, and the town lost the chance of having a hotel forever…

"At least it's a big job for you," Hannah said. "If he hires you to do all the plumbing work?"

"Yes, but I'm not sure I'm up for that kind of thing," Meghan admitted. Not to mention being in close proximity to Quinn for that long, although realistically she knew he'd probably head back to the city or wherever he came from rather than stay here and supervise all the repairs.

"Why not?" Hannah asked. "You could use the money, couldn't you?"

"Yes…" Hell, yes. "But my experience is mainly fixing leaky taps and toilets, installing the odd sink or shower. I haven't done a really big job ever." No one had big jobs around here, and she'd never had the resources to take extra training courses. Her one-year apprenticeship had been in the basics.

"Maybe now's the time," Hannah answered. "Dream big, Meghan."

"Right."

"I'll see you at the talent show on Friday?"

"Wouldn't miss it for the world," Meghan promised. After she'd hung up the phone, she stared out the kitchen window at the stand of pines behind the little ranch house she rented on the edge of town. She could see the silvery glint of the St. Lawrence in the distance, the river a frozen silver ribbon under the moonlight.

She felt tension knot her shoulders and a familiar pain settle underneath her breastbone. Loneliness. She hated admitting it, even to herself, but God help her, even with friends like Hannah and Sam, even with a whole town at her back, she was lonely. At the end of the day it was just her and Polly, and when it came to Polly, it was pretty much just her. Her mother had turned her back years ago and her father, even though he only lived a couple of miles away, couldn't really be counted on, although he did the best he could. Friends helped when they could, but it wasn't the same.

Taking a deep breath, Meghan willed the emotion back. Stupid Quinn Freeman had stirred something up inside her she really didn't need stirring. A memory of how things used to be, so long ago, and a yearning for things now to be different. She wondered, suddenly, if he felt the same. Did he remember his father? He'd said he hadn't remembered anything. Did he miss the family he used to have? She wasn't the only one who had lost something. Quinn had, in fact, lost something far dearer.

With a sigh she turned away from the window and went

to sit with Polly on the sofa.

"*Amazing Wedding Cakes*?" she guessed with a nod towards their TV. Polly loved the Food Network.

"Yes, aren't they beautiful?" Polly said, and then she curled into Meghan, resting her head on her shoulder, and let out a happy sigh.

Meghan stroked Polly's hair and leaned against the sofa, savoring her sister's warmth and trying to treasure this moment of peace—and not to think about Quinn Freeman.

CHAPTER FOUR

QUINN COULDN'T DECIDE if he was looking forward to Meghan O'Reilly returning or not. He'd slept badly; the person in the room next to his had been watching TV until four in the morning, and the walls were thin enough that Quinn had heard nearly every tense word and tire screech of *Ice Road Truckers.*

When he'd finally fallen asleep, he hadn't dreamed of the hotel, and when he woke he realized he was disappointed. Some part of him wanted those dreams, those phantom memories. Maybe they would trigger something and he'd suddenly be given back the first six years of his life.

As for Meghan O'Reilly… she was a gorgeous, irritating, prickly woman, and the accusations she'd flung at him had been totally unfair, but… she was sexy. And spirited. And he found he enjoyed both qualities.

Meghan was all business today as she pulled into the parking lot and then strode into the house, a clipboard under one arm and an army green jacket with O'Reilly Plumbing stitched on the breast pocket. She gave him a brisk hello, declining his offer of instant coffee, and then suggested she go through the hotel and assess any internal water damage before deciding what needed to be done.

"I haven't been upstairs yet," Quinn told her. "I'm not sure the stairs will hold."

"There's only one way to find out, isn't there?" Meghan answered, and strode ahead of him. He followed her, half because he didn't want her falling through the second floor, but also because he was curious about her. And, of course, she wasn't bad to look at, either. The army green work pants she wore clung lovingly to her butt.

He stayed silent while Meghan examined each of the bathrooms downstairs, pointing out rust and corrosion on various pipes.

"I should look upstairs to be thorough," she told him when she'd finished and they were standing in the front hall, the grand staircase stretching above them. Even in the hotel's dim light her eyes looked very bright and blue. Mesmerizing. "But I'd say off the bat, to be safe, you're looking at a complete replumbing. You could patch all these pipes if you wanted to do the bare minimum, but even that would start to add up."

"Right." Quinn forced himself to focus on the practicalities. "So what are we talking about, money-wise?"

"I can't say for sure. I've never done a whole replumbing job before." She tilted her chin, those bright blue eyes glinting defiance, as if she expected him to lay into her for her lack of experience.

"Take your best guess," he said.

Meghan bit her lip. Quinn felt a plunging sensation in his stomach, like someone had reached in a fist and squeezed. Her lips were soft and full and pink and *whoa*. Maybe he should have let her work alone.

"It would depend if you went for PVC or copper piping…" she began and Quinn spread his hands.

"Copper's better, right? Let's go for that." He didn't know why he said that; he suspected Adam was going to want to do the hotel up on the cheap and get rid of it as fast as he could.

"Maybe forty thousand dollars?" she said, and Quinn blinked. For just the plumbing, that was a lot of money. Freeman Enterprises could afford it, no question, but judging by the state of the place now, Adam hadn't spent a dime here in decades. Quinn couldn't see him dropping forty grand on some piping.

"Well, that's a lot," he finally said, and Meghan gave a wry smile.

"If you chose PVC piping you could do it for half the amount. Or if you just want to be shot of the place, patch all the leaks you can see. That should run a couple of grand, max."

"Can you write all this up for me? I'll have to submit it to my brother."

She nodded slowly, her gaze sweeping over his face. Quinn stayed relaxed, even though there was too much assessing knowledge in those arctic-blue eyes. "What do you think your brother will say?" she asked. "About all of this?"

"I don't know." Quinn shrugged, uncomfortable with admitting how much power Adam possessed, and how little he had. He'd accepted the way things were seven years ago, when Adam had spelled it out to him plainly. He'd walked away and told himself he didn't care. Right now that lie was starting to wear thin. "I don't think he's going to go for the copper piping, to be honest," he said.

"Or any piping?" Meghan filled in. The woman was too shrewd for her own good.

"Why do you say that?"

"This hotel was left for twenty years without much done to it. You could sell the place as is, if you really wanted to. You might find a buyer. It wouldn't go for much, but you'd be rid of it, at least." She cocked her head, her mouth compressing. "And it seems like that's what you Freemans want."

He didn't like the way she said *you Freemans*, but he decided to let it go for now. "Do you really think someone will buy it like that?" Quinn asked.

"I'm not sure anyone will buy it, period," Meghan told him frankly. "The real estate market around here isn't exactly hopping, and as for a place this size…" She glanced around the hall, two sets of double doors leading off to huge, mostly empty rooms. "I don't know."

"Neither do I," Quinn said after a moment, as the hotel

creaked and settled around them. "But my brief is just to get estimates. Adam will make the decisions."

"And then you go back where? New York City?"

"To my life, yeah," he answered. "Which isn't here."

Meghan's expression closed up and she turned away. "I'll drop off something to you tomorrow morning," she said. "If you'll be here then?" She glanced over her shoulder, and he saw that glint of challenge in her eyes again. What did she want from him? Some absurd promise to fix this place up and put a shiny red ribbon around it?

"Yes, I'll be here tomorrow," Quinn answered. "And the day after that. I'm going to do the job properly. And *then* I'll go."

She didn't answer, just turned around and kept walking.

He spent the afternoon with Tom Wentworth, a local contractor with an affable manner and a beer belly spilling over his tool belt. Nice as the man was, Quinn preferred looking at Meghan. "Most of the damage is on the surface," he said, "which is the good news. You don't have too much structural repair, but a hell of a lot of interior decorating."

"So the floors aren't rotten?" Quinn asked as the floorboard under him creaked ominously.

"The floorboards may be rotten but the beams underneath aren't," Tom explained. "*That's* the good news." He promised to write an estimate and deliver it in the next few days.

An electrician was coming the day after tomorrow, and

Quinn suspected the place would need a total rewiring. But after he got that estimate, he could file the paperwork with Adam and call it done. He'd never have to set foot in Creighton Falls again.

Funny, but that thought didn't make him feel as relieved as it should have.

Needing a break from the musty atmosphere of the hotel, he grabbed his parka and boots and headed outside. The sun was shining, the snow turning to slush under its warming rays, and in the distance Quinn could see that the frozen river was starting to break up into huge chunks of ice, the water churning blackly below. His stomach tightened and he looked away, choosing to walk away from the river, and up towards the hills.

Once he got past the green, he found an avenue of gracious Victorians in various states of grandeur or decay. Some had been chopped into apartments, others were ramshackle with cars on concrete blocks in the driveway, and a lovely few looked like they ought to—with brightly painted gingerbread and flags flying from the wide, brick-pillared porches. Quinn wondered if he'd lived in one of those houses. The house he'd spent his first six years in had been sold when they'd moved.

He was just starting past the last one when a woman came out on the front porch, shielding her eyes with her hand as she looked straight at him. "Quinn? Quinn Freeman?" she called, her voice cracking, and he froze for a second before slowly turning.

"Yes…?"

"It is Quinn?" she asked, coming down a few steps to squint at him. "You're too young to be Adam and too light-haired to be Jacob. So you must be Quinn. *Quinn.*" Her voice broke and she blinked back tears.

Quinn felt like he'd never seen her before in his life, and yet obviously he must have. "I'm sorry…" he began.

"You don't remember me." She waved a hand in acceptance or perhaps understanding, and fished for a handkerchief from the pocket of her cardigan. "I'm not surprised," she continued as she dabbed her eyes. "I was your family's housekeeper. Janet Pierce."

"And you obviously know who I am." Quinn's gaze swept over the woman; she was tall and spare with her gray hair scraped back into a tight bun. "I'm sorry I don't remember you."

"What little boy remembers the maid?" Janet answered with a huff of laughter. "But it's good to see you. I'm glad you're back." She narrowed her eyes as Quinn stood before her. "I do hope you're back to deal with the hotel?"

Quinn said the only thing fitting in the circumstances. "Yes, ma'am."

"You'd better come in and tell me all about it," Janet Pierce said, and turned around to head back into the house. She glanced over her shoulder when Quinn didn't move. "And I won't take no for an answer. Not after twenty-two years. You might not remember me, Quinn Freeman, but I remember you. You were a terror as a toddler. You drove your mother frantic."

"Not much has changed," Quinn answered with a smile, and mounted the stairs. He stepped inside the house, closing the double glass-paned doors behind him. The house smelled both musty and clean, of lemon polish and lavender and age.

Janet was leading the way back to the kitchen, and so Quinn followed, noting the antique furniture that graced the rooms, the black and white photographs on the walls. He felt as if he'd stepped into a museum.

"This house belonged to my husband's parents," Janet said as she put an old-fashioned copper kettle on top of the large range stove. "I married late, after you all left." She spoke without rancor, but Quinn tensed anyway. After you left. Coming from Meghan, it had felt like an accusation. He didn't know what it was coming from Janet Pierce.

Janet glanced around the comfortable, cozy kitchen with its round table covered in a waxed cloth, sunlight streaming through the windows, with affection. "It worked out well, even though we only had a few years together."

"How long did you work for us?" Quinn asked. He felt as if he were groping in the dark when everyone else had access to the light switch.

"Seventeen years, since before Adam was born," Janet said. "I dandled all three of you on my knee, if you can believe it."

He couldn't. He searched her face, looking for something to jog his memory, but nothing did. She smiled with wry sorrow.

"I can see you don't remember. Maybe it's better that way."

His throat tightened at that statement. "Do you really think so?" he asked, hoping his voice sounded neutral.

"It was a tragedy," Janet said quietly. "A terrible tragedy."

A tragedy that had been his fault. If he hadn't gone out on the ice. If he hadn't fallen in.

"An accident," Janet said firmly, as if she could read his mind, and Quinn managed a stiff smile.

"Right."

In the twenty-two years since his father's death, they'd rarely, as a family, talked about Peter Freeman or anything to do with Creighton Falls. His mother had always found it too painful, and both Jacob and Adam had maintained a stony silence about everything. Quinn knew both of his brothers must have memories, lots of them; Jake had been twelve when their father had died, Adam sixteen. He was the only one with the huge blank, and right now, with this kindly woman staring him full in the face, he felt it unbearably.

"So what are you going to do with the hotel?" Janet asked as the kettle came to a boil and she whisked it off the stove, pouring the water into a teapot. "I hope you like chamomile. It's all I have."

Quinn was pretty sure he wouldn't like chamomile, but he murmured something polite. She gave him a hopeful smile. "Are you going to reopen it?"

"No, I'm afraid not." He seemed to be forever the bearer of bad news. Good thing he was used to disappointing people. "We're selling it."

Janet's shoulders slumped even as she nodded. "I suppose that's to be expected. After all this time..." She sighed. "It would be too much to hope for, to think things might change."

"Considering how we've neglected the place, I think people might be glad to be rid of us for good," he said, and Janet shook her head sorrowfully.

"Better to mend something than throw it away, don't you think?"

"Maybe someone else will buy it and reopen it."

"Maybe, but I think everyone in Creighton Falls would rather a Freeman ran it. The town might not look much to you, but its people are loyal. Fiercely so." She handed him a cup of chamomile tea; Quinn thought it smelled vile but knew he would drink every drop, for Janet's sake.

He took a sip of the tea and nearly gagged. No, he definitely did not like chamomile.

Janet sat at the table, beckoning for Quinn to do the same. "I always thought it was a second tragedy, to leave the way your mother did. She loved it here, you know. Loved the town, the river, the people, all of it."

"Did she?" The words felt squeezed out of his throat. He couldn't imagine it, considering the only memory he had was of his mother hating the place, refusing to let the name of it pass her lips.

"She grew up across down the river, in Clayton. Did you know that?"

"Vaguely," he admitted, abashed. His mother's parents had died when he was a baby.

"Now that's a place that still has its hotels, its tourism and industry," Janet said with a sigh. "But it's closer to the highway too."

"Do you really think reopening the hotel would help Creighton Falls?" Quinn asked.

Janet let out a dry rasp of a chuckle. "I suppose you think the town is past saving."

"Not exactly…"

"I'll admit, it doesn't look its best this time of year, with dirty snow covering everything and the mud still to come. But it's a beautiful place, with the trees and the meadows and everything right on the river—" She stopped suddenly, and Quinn realized she must have seen something in his face. Hell if he knew what. "Oh, Quinn. I'm sorry." She reached over and squeezed his hand, shocking him with the simple touch. "The river must hold such bad memories for you."

"Actually, I don't remember any of it. The… accident." His voice sounded rusty and strange.

"Don't you?" Janet sat back in her seat, eyeing him

thoughtfully. "Maybe that's better, too."

Quinn stared down at his cup of herbal tea, vile that it was. He was afraid of what Janet Pierce might see in his face, in his eyes.

"So why didn't Creighton Falls bounce back?" he asked when he trusted the timbre of his voice.

Janet sighed sadly. "Because your family was the life blood of this town, and when you went, you left a corpse behind." She shook her head. "I know it sounds harsh, but that's the truth of it, I'm sorry to say."

"What did people do?" Quinn asked. "After?"

Janet sipped her tea thoughtfully before replying. "Managed as best as they could, really. Struggled on. The craft shop on the green lasted for a couple of years. The card shop went quicker. But not everybody rolled over when you left," Janet added robustly. "Fiona has started a bakery, and Elsie McGuinness kept the diner going. There's life blood in this town, corpse that it might be. We *try*, Quinn. We all try."

"I'm sure you do." Quinn shifted in his seat. "I'm sorry for what happened," he said after a moment. "But I think the best thing we can do now is sell the hotel and let someone else have a chance."

Janet raised her eyebrows. "Best for whom?" she asked. "Not the best for us, certainly, but more to the point, not the best for you."

Quinn decided not to ask what she meant.

Fifteen minutes later, after having managed to drink the

rest of his tea down under Janet Pierce's concerned and beady eye, Quinn was heading back down the porch stairs, relieved and yet also disappointed to be escaping the older woman's scrutiny. He felt as if he'd let her down, as if he'd let a lot of people down. It was a sadly familiar feeling, but it still got to him, especially here.

"Thank you for the tea," he said, and Janet's lips twitched in a way that made Quinn suspect she'd known he'd had to choke down every sip. He hesitated a second longer and then blurted out the question, "Do you remember what it was like... the hotel... at Christmas?"

Janet's face softened into what Quinn cringingly suspected was pity. "Yes, of course," she said. "It was gorgeous. Your mother oversaw the decorating herself. Fresh evergreen on every mantle, candles in the windows, and red velvet ribbons around the tables with their snow-white cloths. Truly beautiful."

He couldn't keep himself from asking another question. "Was there... was there a Christmas tree? In the front room, by the fireplace?"

Janet nodded, her gaze distant now, lost in memories. "Yes, of course there was. A huge one, at least ten feet tall. Your father cut it down and brought it inside himself every year. It was a family tradition."

And just like that a memory slammed into Quinn, so strong and so clear he nearly staggered. His father's hand on his head, ruffling his hair. The sharp, fresh scent of evergreen, the tinkle of jingle bells on the front door, the feeling of anticipation and happiness…

He sucked in a hard breath, feeling as if he'd been sucker punched. Janet Pierce was gazing at him, a slight frown on her wrinkled face.

"Quinn…?"

"Thank you," he said, and started back down the road. He walked quickly down the street, head tucked low, barely aware of his surroundings that became a blur of sky and street. He walked faster and faster, and then, without even realizing it, he was running. It felt good to have his feet hit the pavement hard, the breath searing his lungs.

He'd finally remembered something, and it didn't feel the way he thought it would. Redeeming, if a little bittersweet. No, this felt… hard. It hurt. It showed him a gaping place inside him that he'd fooled himself into thinking wasn't there.

Quinn sprinted past the hotel, across the village green, and then cut down an alley between the diner and a deserted storefront that led to where some part of him had been needing to go all along. The river.

He sprinted through snow, spattering wet, gray slush onto his jeans, past a park bench and a sign that said no fishing to the riverbank.

It wasn't a particularly wide river, the St. Lawrence, at least not right there. He could see the other side, a haze of gray-green trees, and in the middle a few scattered islands, some barely big enough to stand on. One held a cottage with a weathered dock, another just an old shed.

He looked down at the chunks of ice bobbing in the churning river; the water was black and fathomless, angrily foaming up around them in white frills.

Suddenly he felt physically sick and he doubled over, gasping, shocked by the flash of memory—no more than a choking sensation, a desperate terror—that went through him like a bolt of lightning, flaying his senses. Here was memory. This was what his subconscious had chosen to forget.

He forced himself to straighten, to stare at the jagged blocks of ice, the terrible black water, as a terrible grief reverberated through him, threatening to send him to his knees. And then, with a shuddering breath that was far too close to a sob, he turned and walked away.

CHAPTER FIVE

MEGHAN ENTERED THE Creighton Falls Community Church with a headache and a cherry pie from the Price Chopper five miles toward Watertown. Brenda Wickley took the pie off her, whisking it away to the table creaking with homemade offerings, with a wink Meghan didn't understand until her gaze moved over the crowd assembled for the annual town talent show and then screeched to a stop on a familiar dirty blond head. So Quinn Freeman was still in town, and more to the point, he'd actually come to the talent show.

He was sitting alone, leaning back in a folding chair, one booted foot resting on his other knee, looking relaxed and amused, as if he were just a little bit above it all. Meghan could see everyone around shooting him speculative looks, from the now openly gaping Brenda to the more discreet, darting looks of Hannah and Sam Taylor. Even Billy Kargas was eyeing him curiously. Quinn seemed to take no notice of anyone.

Meghan shrugged out of her jacket, the warmth of the room enveloping her with its stifling yet comfortable familiarity and the pulsing pain that had banded her temples for most of the day starting to recede a little. She'd grown up in this church, had attended awkward teenaged dances and family bingo nights, potluck suppers and endless talent shows, not to mention plenty of Christmas Eve and Easter church services.

A few people waved and others said hello, and Meghan smiled and nodded at them all, even as she started walking towards the seat next to Quinn's.

He turned, his eyebrows rising as she sat down next to him. "Well, hello there." Blatant male appreciation lit his eyes as his gaze roved over her. She'd never been one to gussy up, but she'd made a bit of an effort tonight, with eyeliner, a bright sweater, and skinny jeans. Unable to keep herself from preening a little under Quinn's warm look, Meghan decided it had been worth it. No harm in playing a little. She could use the distraction. It certainly wasn't going to go anywhere. Quinn was going to be out of here in a couple of days, max.

"I didn't think you were planning to stick around."

Quinn's eyebrows arched higher. "It's only been three days."

"You must have got the estimates for all the work by now." She'd sent hers in two days ago. "What's keeping you?"

Quinn glanced away, leaning his elbows on the back of his chair. "Couldn't miss the talent show, could I?"

"Trust me, you could." Meghan settled herself in her

chair, shoving her coat underneath her seat. "Although we locals love it. But doesn't the Big Apple call you back?"

"Is New York City better than Creighton Falls, in your estimation?" he asked, a teasing glint in his hazel eyes. His mouth kicked up at one corner and Meghan's insides sizzled. She didn't know what she felt about Quinn Freeman as a person, but as a man he was definitely sexy. And she was not immune.

"Not in mine," she answered, "but I thought it would be in yours."

"Maybe you thought wrong." He shrugged his own response away as he added, "In any case, I don't live in New York."

"You don't? Where do you live then?"

Another shrug, the movement just as dismissive, as restless. "All over."

"How's that?"

He seemed reluctant to reply, his gaze on the makeshift stage at the front of the church hall. Billy Kargas was testing the microphone and the resulting screech kept him from answering for a few moments anyway. Finally he said, "I've been traveling around for the last couple of years, working where I can."

"What kind of work?"

"Whatever comes my way. Bartending mostly." He flashed her a quick smile. "Great way to see the world."

So basically he was a bum. Meghan couldn't deny that

she was a little disappointed in Quinn's answer, even as she acknowledged that she wasn't all that surprised. He didn't want for money, and from the moment she'd met him his lackadaisical attitude had pointed to a pleasure-seeking lifestyle.

"Must be nice," she finally said, keeping her voice neutral.

"It's been all right," he answered, his gaze flicking away from hers. "What about you? How did you become a plumber?"

"I needed a steady job and plumbing seemed like the best bet." She heard a slight edge to her voice and realized she wasn't just disappointed in Quinn's answer, she was envious. Envious of the freedom and opportunities he no doubt took for granted. "I did an online course when I was seventeen and then I apprenticed to a plumber in Watertown for a year before starting out on my own." She'd been eighteen years old, the breadwinner for her and Polly. Not an easy time.

Quinn's hazel gaze moved slowly over her. "And you're successful."

"I make ends meet." Sometimes only just.

"What about your parents?" he asked. "Are they around? Do they help with Polly?"

"My mother's out in Arizona, and my dad..." She hesitated, not wanting to criticize her father and yet... "He does what he can."

"Must be tough," Quinn said quietly and now Meghan

was the one to shrug and look away.

"It is what it is. Polly works at a supermarket near Water-town. She's not..." Meghan stopped, because she didn't know how to finish that sentence. *She's not hopeless. She's not completely dependent on me. I love her with every breath in my body even though sometimes it's hard.*

"Where is she tonight?"

"She's with my friend, Janet, making cupcakes. Polly loves baking." And Janet had been a godsend over the years, offering to have Polly over when Meghan needed a little downtime. Plenty of people in Creighton Falls had stepped up for her, and it did combat the loneliness and isolation that came with being Polly's sole caretaker. Mostly.

Quinn raised his eyebrows. "Janet Pierce?"

"You know her?"

"Apparently she was my family's housekeeper when I was little. I ran into her the other day. Didn't remember her, though."

"It must be strange," Meghan said slowly. "For so many people to know you without you knowing them back."

"Yeah." He smiled wryly before nodding to Brenda, who was arranging the pies on a side table. "She knows me. She told me tonight that she changed my really messy diaper."

Meghan laughed at that. "Almost everyone in Creighton Falls knows you or at least your family, although not quite in that capacity."

"Do you?" Quinn asked abruptly. "I mean... do you remember… my family?" He held her gaze, and underneath the careless, easy attitude, Meghan sensed a hidden vulnerability that surprised her. Touched her too, if she was honest. He looked like he really wanted to know. Like he really needed to know.

"I remember the hotel being open," she said slowly. "My dad used to do fishing tours for the guests there." And now she was the one feeling vulnerable, as she recalled how simple life used to be. "I remember that your family hosted a Christmas open house for everyone in the town each year. We used to go along. Your mother gave every child a little present, wrapped up with a bow and everything."

"Did she?" He sounded wondering. "I don't remember any of it."

"Nothing?" Meghan asked curiously. "Not even little snatches of things?" It seemed strange to have drawn a complete blank across the first six years of your life. She had plenty of memories from first grade: losing her front tooth, getting her first bike. Holding Polly as a baby, who had been born right before her sixth birthday.

"Nothing at all," Quinn said flatly. His gaze had shuttered, his jaw going tight. "At least… until recently."

Meghan wasn't able to respond because the talent show was starting. Deciding the mood could use a little lightening, Meghan leaned over and whispered in Quinn's ear. "Brace yourself for Creighton Falls' astonishing talent. Trust me, we give *The X Factor* a run for its money."

She hadn't meant to lean quite so close, and her lips were practically brushing his ear. She could smell his aftershave and she had the absurd urge to bury her nose in the warm curve of his shoulder and take a big sniff.

Quinn slanted her a sideways glance, and she could tell from the slight tension in his body that he felt at least some of the same awareness that she did. "Oh? What should I look forward to, then?"

"Billy Kargas," Meghan answered promptly. "He will render you speechless."

His mouth curved in a smile, and now Meghan had the urge to kiss one quirked-up corner. She was close enough to see the glint of a five o'clock shadow on his jaw and she imagined running her fingers against it, feeling that scratchy-smooth sensation of skin and stubble. It had been a long, long time since she'd touched a man like that.

Out of the corner of her eye she saw Hannah Taylor gazing at her with avid interest and regretfully she eased back. Flirting with Quinn Freeman at the town's talent show was a very bad idea. Unless she wanted their marriage announcement in the local paper by tomorrow. Still, it had been fun, at least for a few minutes.

The first act had ambled onto the stage, three farmers with banjo, fiddle, and accordion. The resulting sound was at least lively, if slightly off-kilter, and Quinn gave Meghan a sidelong, knowing glance.

"I see what you mean," he murmured.

"Just wait."

The next act were three would-be ballerinas, the oldest one being only five. The youngest, a two-year-old named Chloe, ran off the stage and buried her head in her mother's lap, refusing to go back on despite many urgings and a round of cheering from the audience. Then came Marie Czartoski, who had dreams, or perhaps delusions, of being an opera singer. She tried out for *America's Got Talent* every year, and wrote up her experiences in the local newspaper. She had yet to get past the first round of auditions.

Half a dozen decent acts followed, and then Billy Kargas lumbered on, a tall man carrying an extra fifty or so pounds, wearing his best red plaid flannel shirt and denim overalls with green suspenders. Meghan had known Billy for her whole life; he'd had a boat, just like her dad, to run fishing tours for guests before the hotel had closed. For the last twenty years he'd been doing what her father did: finding odd jobs where he could and collecting welfare when he couldn't.

Brenda Wickley was on the piano, banging out the basic chords for *The Heart Will Go On*. Only Billy would attempt a Celine Dion song. Meghan leaned over to Quinn again, just to breathe him in one more time. "This will really knock your socks off."

Quinn nodded slowly, his eyebrows raised in expectation, his mouth curving, and Billy began.

QUINN KEPT HIS face pleasantly neutral with effort as Billy launched into his Celine Dion rendition. Quinn didn't think the guy got one note right, but he certainly put his whole heart into it. Around him everyone was listening with rapt attention, as if Billy were the local Pavarotti, and it wasn't until he saw someone suppress a wince that he realized everyone there knew how bad he was. They just didn't want Billy to know it. And he felt a weird, unsettling tug of affection for this hometown of his that still felt like such a strange place, and yet one he might actually want to get to know.

He glanced at Meghan, and saw she was watching Billy as if entranced. She might have joked about him to Quinn, but he knew instinctively that Meghan would clap as hard as everyone else when Billy finished. She was an intriguing mixture of sharpness and courage, spiky defensiveness and heartrending vulnerability. He'd seen it in her eyes when she'd talked about her sister, her absentee parents. He felt it in himself.

Or maybe he was just becoming massively sentimental, because since coming back to Creighton Falls he'd felt... unbalanced. Until he'd stepped foot in that moldering hotel, seen the glint of the river, he hadn't let himself think much about Creighton Falls at all. His family never talked about it. He didn't remember any of it. He'd mentally drawn a line across the first six years of his life and moved on.

Or at least he'd acted as if he had. Pretended to himself

he had. But coming back here was making him realize that he hadn't, not remotely. That there were ghosts in his past, flirting with his memory, making him wonder and wish and grieve. All of which should make him want to hightail it out of this town as fast as possible, except he'd been stupidly reluctant to do that.

And so he'd taken his time to get a few more estimates; he'd ripped up a few carpets and torn off the wallpaper in the lounge just to see what was underneath. And he'd gone to sleep every night half-hoping for another dream about the hotel, half-afraid of what he might remember.

Billy Kargas finished with a screeching flourish, and the entire crowd clambered to their feet to give him a standing ovation. Billy beamed and suggested an encore, but Terence Mills, the minister of the congregation and emcee for the night, told him that they were sadly out of time.

Quinn didn't think he was imagining the silent, collective sigh of relief that went up through the rows of folding chairs.

A couple more acts and the show was over. Terence asked for help folding the chairs before they dug into all the pie on offer. Quinn rose and began to fold his, reaching for Meghan's, who shook her head and folded it herself.

"So how did you get roped in to coming to the talent show, anyway?" she asked.

"A woman stopped by to introduce herself and invite me. It was hard to say no, not that I wanted to."

"A woman?"

"Hannah something...?"

"Hannah Taylor," Meghan finished. "She's new to Creighton Falls, but she loves this town."

"I could tell. She asked me if I was going to reopen the hotel."

"I guess everyone is asking you that."

"Pretty much." Quinn raked a hand through his hair, shaking his head. "I keep telling people, it's not my decision to make."

"Maybe it should be."

He glanced at her, saw the defiant glint in her ice-blue eyes, and tensed. "What is that supposed to mean?"

Meghan shrugged. "You're the one here, aren't you? You're the one who is taking an interest. Why can't you decide to keep it open?"

As if it were that simple. As if Adam or anyone in his family would listen to him for a moment. They hadn't before. *This doesn't concern you, Quinn.* Adam's officious voice, his mother's pleading gaze. *Leave well enough alone.* No, nobody in his family wanted him sticking his nose in the family business. His mother might have asked him to get a few estimates, but it was akin to throwing him a bone. She didn't want him wrestling Adam for control, which was what any bid for more responsibility would end up being.

He shook his head as Meghan continued to stare at him challengingly. "It doesn't work like that."

"Why not? Or do you have another bartending gig in Bali to go to?"

He jerked back, stunned and more than a little insulted by the scorn he heard in her voice. So she thought he was a pretty useless playboy. She wouldn't be the first, and Quinn knew he hadn't done much to contradict the assumption. He'd long ago learned there was no point.

The chairs had all been folded and put away, and people began to migrate towards the table on the side that was laden with pies. Quinn and Meghan fell in with everyone else, and it wasn't until he'd helped himself to a slice of apple toffee pie that he said in a low, terse voice, "Just because my family has money doesn't mean everything is easy."

"I never said it was," Meghan answered as she reached for a paper plate.

"Everyone here seems to think I can snap my fingers and make things happen."

"Maybe because that's how it used to be."

"Yeah, well, it's different now," Quinn said, and he heard the anger in his voice. "I'm different." And without waiting for her reply, he went off with his pie.

MEGHAN WATCHED QUINN shovel his pie into his mouth as if he were starving, wondering what he'd meant when he'd said *I'm different*. Different from whom? His family? His father? This town?

She watched, bemused, as locals started to circle him;

everyone wanted to know what was going on with the hotel, and by coming to the talent show, Quinn had marked himself as fair game. It was open season on a Freeman.

And open season on her too, she realized, as Brenda sidled close to her. "You and the Freeman boy were looking pretty cozy there."

"It's work, Brenda. He asked for an estimate on replumbing the hotel."

"Heard you gave him the replumbing estimate two days ago."

Was *nothing* secret in this town? Meghan sighed and speared a forkful of lemon meringue. "There are still details to be discussed."

"So he *is* thinking of staying around?" There was no disguising the glee in Brenda's voice.

"No…" Too late Meghan realized she'd started a dangerous rumor. She needed to haul it back asap. "No, Quinn's just fixing it up so the Freemans can get the best price for it. That's all, Brenda, honestly."

Brenda fixed her with a glittering, gimlet stare. "Quinn, is it?"

Meghan groaned and rolled her eyes. Sometimes this town felt way too small.

It was getting late, and Janet liked to go to bed early, so Meghan decided to call it a night. She called out a few goodbyes, tossed her paper plate into the trash, and headed out into the darkness.

It was a cold, clear night, and Meghan tipped her head up to the star-scattered sky and breathed in the sharp pine-scented air, grateful, in that moment at least, for the simple, rustic beauty of her hometown. She loved Creighton Falls, always would, even if sometimes she felt stuck.

"Meghan." She tensed as she heard Quinn's voice behind her and she lowered her head to see him emerging him from the church, his hands jammed into the pockets of a parka. She wondered if he was still angry with her, but as he came closer she saw the insouciant glint in his eye, the teasing curve of his lips. Seemed like Quinn had already moved on.

"So, you escaped," she said.

"By the skin of my teeth. Brenda Wickley should work for the CIA."

"She's tenacious."

He shifted where he stood. "I'm not used to a place where everyone wants to know your business."

"Welcome to Creighton Falls."

"Yeah, well." A pause, and the air felt electric. The tiny hairs on Meghan's arms prickled, and not with cold. With expectation. She'd been trying her hardest to deny it, but she'd felt the pull of attraction, of longing, toward this man ever since she'd clapped eyes on him. "I'm leaving tomorrow."

"You are?" She tried to squelch the irrational disappointment she felt. Stupidly, despite her baiting earlier, she'd thought he might stick around a little longer. "Why?"

"Nothing else to do here."

Which is what she'd told him before. "Okay."

Quinn shifted his stance, his gaze turning even and measured. Calculated. "I know the place is a wreck, but do you want to come back to the hotel with me?" Meghan's startled gaze flew to his as he paused deliberately. "For a drink?"

She didn't have a lot of bedroom experience, but she'd been around the block enough to know what Quinn was suggesting, and it wasn't just a friendly nightcap.

She licked dry lips, her heart starting to hammer. No one had ever propositioned her so blatantly before, unless you counted Todd Cybalski's invitation to go fishing with him, with a loud guffaw and a gesture to his crotch. Charming.

"But you're leaving tomorrow."

He lifted his chin, his intent gaze never leaving hers. "Exactly."

So a one-night stand. No strings, no promises, no emotion. Just the sheer physical pleasure of the thing. And Meghan knew she was tempted, maybe more than she should be. No one was outside; they could leave now, walk to the hotel, and she could sneak back later to her truck with no one in Creighton Falls the wiser. They could explore this attraction, work out some stress in the best way possible. Or so she supposed. It had been a long time since she'd been even close to naked with a man.

Quinn raised his eyebrows. "Well?"

"I have to pick up my sister."

"Can't you be a little late?"

She licked her lips again and hitched her bag higher on her shoulder. "How late?"

He shrugged. "You tell me." His smile was slow and wicked as he murmured, "A lot can happen in an hour."

Heat flared through her and images danced in her mind. Images of Quinn Freeman's golden skin, his kissable lips, his perfectly defined chest. Then her stomach cramped and she started to feel sick. What the hell was she thinking? Having a quickie in an abandoned hotel with a stranger?

Was that what her life had become, that all she could do was snatch a moment's fleeting, sordid happiness? Or maybe an hour of it.

Quinn must have seen the change in her expression, felt her withdrawal, for he slid his keys out of his pocket and jangled them in his hand. "Maybe not, eh?" he said, and started to walk away.

Meghan stared at his retreating back in both shock and outrage. It was so easy for him, both the picking up and the discarding. The fact that he could walk away so easily, whistling as he went, made her realize she'd been right to refuse his offer.

Not that he'd actually given her a chance.

"Have a nice life, Quinn Freeman," she called, and his stride slowed for a second. "Since I most likely won't see you again."

He turned his head so his face was in profile. "You too, Meghan O'Reilly," he said, and then he kept walking.

Meghan watched him walk all the way across the green and into the hotel before she turned around. She let out a gusty sigh, her breathing forming a puff of frosty air, as she battled a dozen different emotions. Annoyance. Outrage. Anger. Hurt. And disappointment, because now that he was gone, she almost wished she'd taken Quinn Freeman up on his offer.

CHAPTER SIX

"**Y**OU'VE BEEN *WHERE?*"

Quinn sprawled in a club chair in his brother's office, noting the color that had surged into Adam's face. "If you don't learn to chill, you're going to have a stroke before you're forty."

"Why the hell were you in… *there,* Quinn?" Adam demanded. He couldn't even say the words Creighton Falls.

"Because our mother asked me to go," Quinn answered shortly. "Did you know the hotel is about to be condemned?" He raised his eyebrows, waiting, while Adam turned away and busied himself with some papers on his desk. A floor-to-ceiling picture window gave Quinn an uninterrupted view of midtown, the sky cloudless and blue, the world below a hive of activity, dark-suited business people walking briskly to important places. "Did you?" he pressed, and Adam let out an impatient sigh.

"I might have been sent something about it."

Irritation prickled along his skin and Quinn leaned forward. "Sent something? It was damn careless of you, Adam, to neglect—"

"You're going to talk to me about careless, Quinn?" Adam let out a disbelieving huff of laughter. "Really?"

Quinn sat back in his seat, his mouth compressed. "There's a difference between careless and carefree."

"And of course you would make that distinction."

Quinn let the jibe pass. He'd chosen his lifestyle because of Adam, and his brother knew that full well. "Regardless, it's our family's responsibility to—"

"You don't know the meaning of the word," Adam snapped. "You've been playing at being a beach bum for the last seven years, without a thought for anyone or the family business."

"And why is that?" Quinn snapped. "Because you haven't wanted me involved. You made that abundantly clear." And Jake and his mother had backed him up. Even now, eight years later, the memory burned.

"You aren't exactly qualified," Adam returned evenly. "A college dropout—"

"I wasn't a dropout the last time I came to you with a suggestion," Quinn said coldly. A tense silence followed, and then Adam looked away.

"I only did what our mother asked me to do," Quinn said when he trusted his voice to sound level. "I'm relaying this information on her behalf, Adam. I've made a list of repairs the hotel needs—"

"How kind of you." Adam sat down hard in his seat, pulling his laptop toward him. Quinn watched him for a few moments, noting the lines of tension that bracketed his brother's mouth, the scattering of gray at his temples. His brother was a total workaholic. He was thirty-eight years old and Quinn thought it quite likely that he'd burn out before he was fifty. Either that or work himself to death. But maybe that was what Adam wanted.

"So what are you going to do about the hotel?"

Adam didn't even look up from his laptop. "That's none of your concern."

"Considering I spent the better part of a week there looking at the place, I think it is."

Briefly Adam glanced up. "All right, so you called in a couple of contractors. *Thank you.* But it doesn't give you the right to make any decisions."

"I've never had that right, have I?" Quinn could feel the anger coiling tighter and tighter inside him. He'd leaned forward in his chair, and his fists were clenched. Besides the tight set of his jaw, Adam's expression hadn't changed. "You refused to give it to me."

"Our father appointed me as CEO, Quinn."

"Trust me, you don't need to remind me of that fact." Sighing heavily, Quinn leaned back in his chair. What was the point of going over old ground? Adam would never change. "Why can't you just tell me what you're going to do?"

Adam pressed his lips together, his eyes flicking up to Quinn and then back to his computer screen. "I'll talk to

Mom," he finally said. "See what she wants to do."

"I already know what she wants to do," Quinn answered, "because she told me. She wants to sell it—"

"Fine," Adam cut him off. "Then I'll sell it."

Which brought them right back to the beginning of the conversation. Quinn gritted his teeth. "Fine. But it needs work before it's put on the market, Adam. That's what I've been trying to tell you. That's why I went up there." He reached for the papers he'd brought. "I've got estimates on all the building repairs. The structure is sound, but it needs a lot of carpentry repairs, and a complete replumbing and rewiring—"

"Replumbing and rewiring?" Adam raised his eyebrows. "That's got to cost close to a hundred grand."

"We have the money."

"Why would I spend that kind of money on that wreck?" Adam demanded. "I want to get rid of the place, not gussy it up. I'll sell it as is, for however much someone's willing to spend on it."

"Which will be pennies, considering all the work it needs."

"Fine, then I'll take pennies. Better to have it off our hands." Adam's expression tightened, his lips firming into a hard line. "We should have sold it years ago."

"Why didn't you, then?"

He shrugged. "Mom didn't want to."

Quinn thought about how Janet Pierce had said his

mother had loved Creighton Falls. It was bizarre to think about now, but it made him understand why his mother might have held onto the hotel as long as she had. It was hard to let go of a dream, a memory. A hope. And he didn't like the thought of selling the hotel, even though he could see the sense in it. He might be starting to remember his life in Creighton Falls, but as a family they needed to let go of it.

Quinn took a deep breath. "Adam, I don't think you're going to get many buyers without doing some basic repairs to the place."

"All I need is one."

"Fine, I don't think you're going to get any buyers. You've at least got to clean the place up, get the rotten furniture out—"

Adam's nostrils flared, his mouth pinching. "You're the expert now, are you?"

"More than you are in this case," Quinn retorted, even though he knew they were both sounding childish now. Seemed like he and his brothers couldn't keep themselves from it.

Adam sighed and pushed back from the desk. "What do you want me to do, Quinn? Sink a hundred grand into this wreck, knowing we'll never get that out of the sale price?" Quinn didn't answer and Adam nailed him with a hard gaze. "What is it that you actually want?"

Hell if he knew. Quinn looked away, trying to marshal his thoughts. "I don't want you to just walk away from the hotel. From the town. If you went up there, if you saw what I saw…" If he'd seen and heard and felt the disappointment and sadness coming from everyone in Creighton Falls, if he'd realized how much the hotel had meant to them…

Well, being Adam, he probably wouldn't change his mind.

"Since you seem so keen on the place," Adam said, an edge to his voice, "why don't you deal with it? You want some responsibility? Fine. Take some."

Quinn's gaze widened. "Do you mean that?"

"Get the place ready to sell," Adam ordered. "And don't spend a dime more than you have to."

"What about the replumbing, the rewiring-"

"I'll give you ten grand to improve the place. And then I'm selling it." Adam turned back to his laptop, and Quinn knew the conversation was closed.

SPRING CAME SLOWLY to upstate New York. Mainly it came in mud, rivers of the stuff, as the snow melted and the river was freed from its prison of ice. Still, there was a beauty to be had in a blue sky, in the crocuses that peeked their bright, fragile heads between clumps of leftover snow, in the barest hint of warmth in the cold, still air.

Meghan climbed into her truck after dropping Polly for her carpool ride into Watertown. Polly took the car with a neighbor, Betty, who worked in a laundromat, and then brought her home again most days. If Meghan was out that way, she'd pick Polly up. It worked, mostly, and that was all Meghan aimed for these days.

She tried to suppress the wash of worry she felt whenever she thought about Polly's care, and the bitterness about how her parents had just walked away from one of their children. She loved her sister dearly, and that deep-rooted seed of resentment always made her feel guilty. How could she begrudge Polly anything? She was her *sister,* full of fun and brimming with love, difficult and temperamental and forever a child. But she was *Polly,* and Meghan loved her. She wouldn't change her if she could. She just wished she had someone in her life to share the burden sometimes.

Sighing, Meghan started up the truck. Truth was she'd been in a bit of a funk ever since a certain Freeman left town two weeks ago. Stupid of her to feel that way, since he wasn't coming back and he'd only been offering a night anyway.

But what a night it could have been.

Impatient with herself, Meghan banged her hand on the steering wheel. "What's wrong with you?" she demanded, her voice sounding loud in the truck's cab. "You deserve more than a one-night stand."

Trouble was she wasn't sure she was going to get any more than that. How many men wanted to sign up to a lifetime of care of a mentally disabled adult? How many men in Creighton Falls did *she* want to sign up with, anyway? The answer, for the last ten years, had been zero. The one she'd suggested it to had walked away easily enough.

Meghan drove by the hotel, automatically slowing as she had every morning and night since Quinn had left, to check if anything had changed. The place still looked like one single breath might blow it all down. Windows shuttered or gaping, gingerbread rotting off, porch deeply bowed. It looked exactly the same.

Then she saw the truck in the parking lot. Meghan slammed on the brakes, her heart stuttering in her chest. She wasn't sure why she suddenly felt breathless with an awful mixture of anxiety and hope. So there was a truck there. Quinn had probably arranged for someone to come in and start the repairs. He hadn't contacted her about the replumbing, but that didn't mean too much. He could have easily found a plumber from Watertown or further afield. He probably had, considering the way they had parted.

Meghan craned her neck but she couldn't see anyone, just a run-of-the-mill Ford truck that looked as beat up as anyone else's around here, a far cry from Quinn's Beamer.

Trying to ignore the disappointment that weighed her down like she'd swallowed a bucket of lead, Meghan drove on.

Two hours later she was taking apart Fiona Denham's toilet, trying to figure out what was causing the clog. One of the joys of being a plumber.

From the front room she could hear Fiona chatting to customers; a couple of years ago she'd bought the old cheese factory, long in disuse, and turned it into a bakery. Amazingly for Creighton Falls, the place was a success.

"So are you staying long?" Fiona's voice drifted down the hall, and Meghan tensed when she heard the answer.

"Until the work is done."

It couldn't be. But that low, easy voice was so familiar. She'd been hearing it in her dreams for two weeks. *A lot can happen in an hour.*

"And then what?" Fiona asked. Meghan leaned forward, straining her ears for the reply.

"Then we sell, hopefully to someone who can turn it into something good for this town."

It *was* Quinn. Meghan was halfway down the hall before she stopped. What on earth was she going to do, barrel into the bakery and give him a hug? The terms they'd parted on had been pretty final. She had no idea what she would say to him now, or what he would say to her.

And yet she was glad he was back.

Meghan tiptoed back down the hall and continued working on the toilet. She heard Fiona call goodbye and the door open and close. Her shoulders sagged a little and she let out a rush of breath. He'd left.

Twenty minutes later she came into the bakery; Fiona was just putting some fresh wheat loaves, golden and perfect, in the display case.

"It smells a lot better in here," Meghan said, and Fiona wrinkled her nose.

"Is the toilet fixed?"

"Yes. One of your customers didn't read the sign about not flushing sanitary products."

Fiona made a face. "Ew. Sorry."

"All part of the job."

She shook her head, smiling. "So it is. Do you like it, Meghan? Being a plumber?"

"It pays the bills."

"I know, but…"

Meghan shrugged. "I like fixing things." Because there was so much in her life that couldn't be fixed. "Was that a Freeman I heard in here awhile ago?" Hopefully her voice sounded casual.

"Quinn Freeman. Remember he was here a couple of weeks ago?"

"Yes…" Meghan made it sound as if she was only vaguely aware of that fact, and Fiona narrowed her eyes.

"Weren't you two chatty at the talent show? And you gave him a replumbing estimate?"

Busted. Why did she even try in this town? "That's right."

Fiona nodded knowingly. "Uh-huh. Well, he's back, and he's going to do as much of the repair work as he can himself."

"Himself? He couldn't even turn off the water valve." And neither could she have, without a wrench.

Fiona shrugged. "I don't know about that. But he's here for a couple of weeks at least, probably more."

"Really?" She focused on pulling on her coat, not wanting to meet Fiona's gaze. Not trusting the expression on her face. A couple of *weeks*. She hadn't expected that. She didn't know how to feel about that. Would he make his offer again? Did she want him to?

"He's a good-looking guy," Fiona remarked. "Very sexy."

"He's blessed with Freeman genes," Meghan answered with a shrug.

"Are all the brothers that hot?"

"I don't actually know," she admitted. "I haven't seen them since they were little." Fiona had moved to the town five years ago; she hadn't grown up with the Freemans' legacy the way Meghan had.

"Well, it'll be nice to have one of them around," Fiona said as she shut the display case. "There aren't too many men in this town who are that easy on the eyes."

No, there definitely weren't. The good ones left or were snapped up straight out of high school. Briefly Meghan thought of Ben Campbell, her one attempt at a serious romantic relationship. He'd upped and left along with her mother; at nineteen he hadn't wanted to sign up for what Meghan had been offering. A lifetime commitment, and she hadn't just meant marriage. But she and Polly were a package deal, always would be. Nothing was going to change that, which was why marriage or even a long-term relationship had been off the cards for a while.

But a one-night stand?

It was something worth thinking about, now that Quinn Freeman was back in town. If he revisited his offer... well, maybe then so would she.

That afternoon she drove slowly by the hotel, debating whether to pull into the parking lot or not. She had an hour before Polly would be home.

A lot can happen in an hour.

Meghan pulled into the parking lot, next to the beat-up truck. She spared her reflection a glance in the rearview mirror; she looked okay but after a day working on people's sewage systems and leaky sinks, she probably didn't smell too great. Nothing she could do about that.

She took a deep breath and slid out of the truck's cab. The door to the kitchen was ajar, and she pushed it open with the flat of her hand as she called inside, "Hello? Anybody home?"

No one replied, but in the distance she could hear the racket of what sounded like someone chopping wood. Her heart starting to hammer, she stepped inside.

CHAPTER SEVEN

I T FELT GOOD to break things. Quinn had shed first his coat and then his shirt as he swung the ax over his head and brought it down hard on the remains of a sagging sofa. The thing splintered apart, a mess of rotting wood and moldy fabric. Useless, or so the furniture restorer who had come in yesterday had told him. The few pieces she'd deemed salvageable had been taken away to her workshop in Albany that morning. The rest was destined for the dump, and Quinn was enjoying working out his frustrations on the furniture.

Damn Adam and his fussy, parsimonious ways. He'd put ten grand in a checking account for Quinn's use, and then refused to discuss the matter. Never mind that the hotel needed ten times that amount to make it sellable. Never mind that they had a duty to the place, to the town, that Quinn was only just starting to understand and knew his brother never would. Adam had never wanted to give Quinn any responsibility, didn't trust him with an inch, never mind even a modicum of the family business. Why should Quinn have expected things to be different now? They never had been.

And never mind that after twenty-four hours in this town, he felt the weight of expectation settle on him, an uneasy burden. People wanted him to take charge, do things, and he wasn't used to that. Wasn't sure what to do with it. After years of expecting to be a disappointment, it felt strange to measure up. How long before the good people of Creighton Falls realized their mistake?

Whack. He brought the ax down again and then kicked the broken pieces toward the growing pile in the corner of the room. So, fine. He had ten grand and a lot of elbow grease. He could make this work. He could clean up this place and make it sellable, give Creighton Falls a fighting chance. That was the least he could do; it was all he could do.

"Whoa."

The voice coming from behind him had him whirling around, the ax still in his hands. Meghan O'Reilly stood there, one hand held up as if to ward him off. She looked gorgeous, tough and sexy in her army-green work shirt and pants, her hair pulled back in a messy ponytail. Quinn felt himself start to grin. No matter how things had ended between them after the talent show, he was glad to see her. Really glad.

"Hey."

She nodded toward the splintered wood at his feet. "I thought you were fixing the place up, not destroying it."

"Yeah. Well." He glanced down at the mess with a wry grin. "This furniture is rotten and needs disposing of."

Meghan cocked her head, ice-blue eyes scanning his face, one hand on her hip. "You're taking that to an extreme, don't you think?"

His grin widened. "Yeah. Maybe. But the sofas are too big to drag outside by myself, and frankly it feels good to swing an ax." He watched as her gaze dipped down to his bare chest and then up again. Saw pink bloom in her cheeks. Well, would you look at that. Meghan O'Reilly could blush. He found he liked the fact. Liked it even better that it was the sight of his bare chest that had put the color in her face.

She shifted her stance, folding her arms. "So why did you come back?"

"To fix the place up."

She arched an eyebrow. "By yourself? What were the estimates for?"

He grimaced, his heated conversations with Adam replaying through his mind. "They were for my brother."

"The one with the purse strings."

"That's him." He heard the edge of irritation in his voice and he swung the ax again at the sofa; it sank into soft, rotting wood. He hated having to admit how powerless he was when it came to his brother.

"So what did your brother do with the estimates?"

"Tossed them in the trash, more or less." Quinn sucked in a quick, measured breath. He wasn't going to run his family down, not here. Last thing they needed was this town having even more of a reason to resent the Freemans. "But he did give me free rein to do what I could myself, and so here I am."

Meghan gazed at him, her arms still folded, the expression in her eyes assessing. "You're going to try to do the replumbing and rewiring yourself?"

"Do I look crazy?"

"I'm not sure." Her gaze swept him up and down, making him tingle. Meghan might have turned him down before, but she'd been tempted then and now he wondered what her reply would be if he made his offer a second time. Wondered if he'd make it. He didn't want his time in Creighton Falls to become more complicated than it already was… and yet some things could be so wonderfully, deliciously simple.

He just didn't know if Meghan O'Reilly was one of them.

"I'm going to do the carpentry work myself. I do have some basic experience in that kind of thing."

"Do you?" She sounded politely incredulous.

Quinn gritted his teeth. "I'm not as much of a useless rich boy as you seem to think I am. I've done a lot of odd handyman type jobs over the years."

"And the electrics and plumbing? What are you going to do about those?"

"I'm still deciding." Quinn kicked the splintered, rotted wood over to the corner of the room, where a pile was already heaped. "I have ten grand to spend on both, so we're looking at a lot of patch jobs."

"Ten grand. That's what your brother allotted for this?"

"Yep." He kept his eyes on the pile of wood, not wanting to see the disappointment or disbelief he suspected would be in Meghan's face.

"Well," she finally said on a sigh, "it's better than nothing."

Quinn risked a glance upward, found a smile as he felt a funny little pulse of relief. "Yeah," he said. "It is."

"You bought a new truck. Or rather, an old one."

"Five hundred bucks from a farmer outside Booneville. I figured the Beamer wasn't necessary."

"Smart move, especially since mud season is starting."

"Mud season?"

"Otherwise known as spring." Her gaze dipped to his chest again and then right back up. "So where are you staying, since you're here for a couple of weeks?"

His eyebrows rose even as a smile played about his mouth. "How do you know I'm here for that long?"

"Oh. Uh." A proper blush, like a crimson tide, washed over her face. "Fiona Denham told me."

"Ah. Gossip travels faster here than the Internet."

"That's not actually saying that much."

"True." Quinn nudged a piece of wood toward the pile with his foot. "Well, you're right. I'm in Creighton Falls for a couple of weeks at the least, and I'm staying right here."

Meghan's mouth dropped open. "In the hotel?"

"Yep."

"But it's…"

"Damp? Disgusting? Decrepit? Right on all three."

"It's not livable, Quinn."

"The room behind the kitchen is. I've cleaned it out. It's mostly dry and thanks to your trusty patch, I can run the water. I have a camp stove that runs on a propane tank. I'm good."

She was shaking her head, as if to deny everything he'd said. "But… why not a hotel?"

"This is a hotel."

A smile lurked in her eyes, made Quinn feel that punch of attraction in his belly. "You know what I mean."

"Yeah, I think I do." He swiped a strand of hair from his eyes, keeping his voice light and easy. "Contrary to what you seem to believe, I'm used to roughing it."

"When?" The word was a challenge.

"I've spent a lot of time traveling," Quinn answered. "And it wasn't in five-star hotels."

"No?"

"Well, not always," he amended with a deliberate grin. "I'm actually more of a Lonely Planet kind of guy." He met her gaze with a challenge of his own. "But then you don't really know me."

"Maybe I don't," Meghan agreed after a moment. She was still giving him that assessing look, but this time he didn't think he came up quite so short. "But you can't eat all your meals on a camp stove."

"There's also the fine establishment across the green."

Meghan rolled her eyes. "You can't eat all your meals there either. You'd die of heart disease before the week was out. Although I do recommend the double cheeseburger with extra bacon."

"That's dinner tonight, then."

"Why don't you come to dinner at my house?" Meghan blurted. And then blushed again. Quinn stared at her, trying to take her measure. What did she want from him? Was this a friendly offer, or something more? "With me and Polly," Meghan clarified. "Since you're going to be staying in Creighton Falls. We might as well be friends."

Might as well…? Quinn could think of something else they *might as well* be, but he didn't look a gift horse in the mouth. He didn't turn free food down, either. And he wanted to see Meghan again, no matter how complicated it turned out to be. "Okay. Thank you."

"Tomorrow night?"

"Sure, just tell me where you live."

Her cheeks were still fiery as she wrote down the details, took his cell number, and then hightailed it out of there. Quinn grabbed his shirt, rubbing the sweat from his body as he wondered just what Meghan O'Reilly wanted from him.

MEGHAN SLAMMED THE oven door closed and wiped her

hands on her jeans, trying to squash the nerves that were writhing around in her belly like a nest of grumpy snakes. Polly wasn't helping; since Meghan had gotten home, she'd been flitting about, caught between excitement and anxiety, no doubt picking up on Meghan's tension.

Already Polly had broken two plates in her eagerness to help set the table; she'd begun to have a meltdown when Meghan had put the store-bought apple strudel out of reach, and then Meghan had broken down and given her sister a bowl of ice cream instead. Fifteen minutes later Meghan realized what a mistake that was, as the sugar hit Polly's bloodstream and she started careening around the living room.

Meghan put a recorded episode of *Amazing Wedding Cakes* on the TV, and Polly finally seemed to settle, her gaze glued to the screen. What had she been thinking, inviting Quinn over for dinner?

The trouble was, Meghan knew she hadn't been thinking. The invitation had popped out of its own accord so both of them had been left blinking in surprise. Maybe she'd been distracted by the sight of his bare chest. It had been a long time since she'd seen that much muscular definition. Meghan's focus had been on not ogling, but she didn't think she'd managed it.

Did Quinn think this was a booty call? How was he going to cope with the chaos of Meghan's home, Polly's hyperactivity and inappropriate questions and all the rest of it? How was *she?*

Quinn was due in five minutes and Meghan hadn't changed or even looked in a mirror. God only knew how awful she looked. With one last check for the lasagna in the oven and another smiling glance at Polly, who was curled up on the sofa, Meghan hurried to her bedroom. She yanked off her work clothes and reached for a not-too-clingy sweater and a pair of jeans. Last thing she wanted was for Quinn to think she was trying too hard, or even at all.

She yanked a brush through her hair, put on some lipstick and then scrubbed it off, and then the doorbell rang. Polly scrambled off the sofa.

"It's Quinn!" she called excitedly. Meghan had explained to Polly who Quinn was, leaving out the unfortunate episode in the bar in Watertown. Knowing Polly, she'd probably forgotten all about it. As affectionate as she could be, she'd never been good at recalling faces; the doctors had said it was part of her condition, and why she sometimes seemed to disconnect emotionally. In a way it was a blessing; Polly had weathered the abandonment of both her parents more easily as a result.

Polly reached the front door before Meghan did, flinging it open and squealing hello.

"Hey there, Polly." Quinn smiled but Meghan saw a wariness enter his eyes. She didn't know whether it was because her sister was strange, or simply that he was remembering their last difficult meeting and hoping not to have a repeat.

"*Quinn!*" Polly threw herself at Quinn who caught her in his arms, nearly dropping the bottle of wine he'd brought. Meghan took it off him and eased Polly away at the same time.

"Let him come in, Poll."

Reluctantly Polly stepped back and Quinn came in their house. Instantly Meghan was aware of how small and cluttered it was. She'd tried to make a home there for her and Polly; she'd sanded and rewaxed the floorboards, and painted the walls a soothing sage green, took her care in choosing the furniture and prints on the walls. But even so, the room was small; the battered sofa was jammed up against the wall, the TV balanced on top of a bookcase overflowing with tattered paperbacks. And everything, carefully chosen or not, was cheap, either secondhand or bargain basement. She saw Quinn glance around the room, his face expressionless, and she felt an internal cringing of embarrassment. No matter what he'd said about roughing it, he had to be used to Manhattan townhouses and gorgeous villas on the beach. Didn't the Freemans own about five houses?

"Come on in," she muttered, and led the way to the kitchen at the back, which was at least brighter than the living room, with windows overlooking a stand of trees, the river visible beyond. Polly, the initial excitement over, had already drifted back to the TV. That was standard Polly, to veer suddenly between over-exuberance and indifference.

Quinn came into the kitchen, his gaze moving to the view of twilight settling softly over the river, the water gleaming darkly under the violet-shadowed sky. Meghan saw something flash in his eyes before he turned to her with a deliberate smile.

"Nice place."

She let out a little laugh. "Not really."

"Better than mine," he answered with a smile.

"At the moment."

"Ever, actually. I've never owned a house."

"Never?"

He shook his head. "Too busy traveling."

Which was a timely reminder of what Quinn Freeman's life was really like. Still, he looked good standing in her kitchen, faded jeans hugging his butt and thighs, a forest green Henley shirt worn to softness drawing attention to the chest she hadn't been able to stop looking at yesterday. His hair was tousled and stubble glinted on his jaw. He looked good enough to eat with a spoon.

"Right," Meghan said and opened the oven to needlessly check on the lasagna. "So where were you last?"

"Thailand."

"Nice." She could only imagine. She glanced at him, saw his gaze move once more to the window and then back again. "What made you want to travel so much?"

He jammed his hands in the pockets of his jeans, giving a shrug. "I wanted to see the world."

It was a pat answer, and Meghan felt there was more to be said. To understand. She braced her hip against the kitchen counter. "You don't have to live a nomad's life to see the world."

"It's one way of doing it." His voice was low and easy but she still sensed a hint of defensiveness from him, and she wondered at it.

"True. But it's a choice, isn't it?" she returned. "A whole way of living your life."

"I guess it is."

"You never wanted to put down roots? Do the nine to five?"

"Not really. But in any case I have years left for that."

"True." Her meant-to-be-fun twenties felt as if they'd passed her by, working as many hours as she could and taking care of Polly. No weekend trips to Florida or jet-setting around Europe; no late nights in Watertown, even. But she wasn't about to throw a pity party about it. She was annoyed that the emotion so much as flickered on the edge of her mind. She'd never regret stepping up and taking care of Polly. *Never.*

"I hope you like lasagna," she said.

"Love it."

She took the lasagna out of the oven, and Quinn brought the bottle of wine to the table. A few minutes later they were all seated, with Polly having reluctantly turned off the TV.

Meghan started dishing out the lasagna and Quinn did

the same with the salad and bread. It felt very cozily domestic to have the three of them seated around the table, eating a simple meal, darkness gathering outside and making the house feel bright and warm. Meghan had never asked a guy back home before, never shared a meal like this, simple as it was. She still was in shock that she'd asked Quinn.

"Why is your hair different colors?" Polly asked Quinn in her abrupt way, and he raised his eyebrows.

"Different colors? How so?"

"Some parts are blond and some parts are brown. It looks funny."

Meghan winced at her sister's bluntness but Quinn took Polly's question with the same seriousness she'd asked it. "The blond parts are that color because I've been in the sun."

"Or in a hair salon?" Meghan couldn't keep from suggesting, and Quinn drew back, almost comically affronted.

"You think I have my hair highlighted in some salon?"

"It looks a little too artful to be natural."

He shook his head, grimacing in disgust. "It's just the sun." He glanced at Polly, giving her a wink. "Trust me."

"Do I know you?" Polly asked, frowning, and Meghan held her breath, hoping Polly wouldn't remember the whole wretched bar scene. That would be difficult to explain.

"You do now." With everyone served, Quinn dug into his food. "So, Polly, you work in Watertown?"

She nodded, puffing her chest out. "At the Stop and Shop."

"Do you like it?"

"I like talking to people. I bag the groceries."

Quinn nodded. "That must be interesting, meeting all the different people who shop there."

"I like the moms the best."

"They're the friendliest?"

"They talk to me the most."

Meghan listened to this exchange with her heart flip-flopping in her chest. Quinn was taking Polly seriously without treating her like a child. Not many people knew how to do that, and yet Quinn made it seem effortless. Natural.

He turned to her. "This is delicious."

"It's not much—"

"Don't put yourself down. The house, the food. It's all great."

Which put a great big lump in her throat. She wasn't used to praise. She reached for her glass, which Quinn had filled with wine, and took a needed sip. "Thank you," she said after she'd swallowed, and Quinn smiled.

The rest of the meal passed with relative ease; Polly fired off a few random questions—Why do you smell like trees? Why did you come here?—which Quinn handled in his familiar, easy way.

After dinner Polly returned to *Amazing Wedding Cakes* and Quinn helped Meghan clear the table. She'd just been about to let him off the hook when he rolled up his sleeves and took his place at the sink. She stared at him in surprise.

"What?" he asked. "You think I can't wash dishes?"

"I didn't think you'd want to wash dishes."

Quinn reached for a plate. "Bring it on."

He washed and she dried in companionable silence, the only sounds the clink of cutlery and china and the tinny sounds of the TV from the other room. Again Meghan acknowledged how domestic this was, how simple and yet how poignant. She'd been alone a long time.

She'd just dried the last plate when she decided she should draw the evening to a close. "Thank you for helping with the cleanup. I need to help Polly get ready for bed…"

Quinn didn't take it as the time-to-leave cue that she'd intended it to be. He shrugged, the movement relaxed and easy, his gaze resting on hers. "I can wait."

Meghan's heart turned over and her breath shortened. Wait for what? What was going on here? What did she *want* to go on here? She didn't know the answers to those questions yet, but neither did she want the evening to end.

Quinn's gaze remained on hers, a faint smile on his face, his hands loosely tucked into the back pockets of his jeans. Meghan took a careful breath and then nodded.

"Okay," she said, and went to find Polly.

CHAPTER EIGHT

I T ONLY TOOK a few minutes to get Polly through her bedtime ritual—teeth brushed, face washed, pajamas. She could do it herself, but it made things go faster if Meghan chivvied her along.

Now Meghan sat on the edge of Polly's bed, smoothing the candy-pink bedspread as her sister snuggled down.

"Is Quinn still here?"

"Yes."

Interest lit Polly's eyes briefly. "Is he sleeping over?"

Heat flashed through Meghan and with effort she kept her expression neutral. "No, Poll. He'll go home soon."

"Will he come back? I like him."

Her heart twisted within her at Polly's simple honesty. She had no idea how to lie or dissemble; what you saw with Polly was what you got. It was a wonderful, if sometimes trying, quality. "I'm sure he will sometime."

"When?"

Another one of Polly's qualities was her dogged persistence. She'd keep asking Meghan until she gave her a definite date. "We'll see him on the weekend," Meghan said, because she figured they could run into him if need be.

"Good." Polly snuggled down deeper under the covers. Meghan remained for a few minutes as she always did, humming softly and stroking Polly's hair. Was this what it felt like to have a child? It was a question she'd often asked herself, because the overwhelming love she felt for Polly was both a privilege and a burden. Did all mothers feel that way? Did they feel trapped and treasured at the same time?

It could take Polly hours to drift off, and so Meghan switched on the white noise machine that helped soothe her to sleep. Some nights, when she was really tired, she just stretched out next to her sister and they fell asleep together. Eventually Meghan made it back to her own bed. Tonight, however, she had someone waiting for her.

Meghan ducked into her own bedroom across the hall to fluff her hair, add a slick of lipstick, rub it off again, and then, just in case, spritz a little deodorant and perfume in the relevant places. Then she took a deep breath and headed out to the living room.

Quinn was sprawled on the sofa, boots off, hair rumpled, watching a recorded episode of *Amazing Wedding Cakes.* He glanced up as Meghan came into the room, his hooded gaze making her feel like he knew exactly what she'd been up to with lipstick and perfume—and why.

He nodded toward the TV. "These things are pretty incredible."

"The cakes? Yeah." Meghan perched on the edge of the

sofa, as far away from Quinn as she could possibly get without being either rude or obvious. She was feeling strung out with nerves, everything in her on edge. "Polly likes baking shows."

"This cake is actually a model of Versailles. Who *does* that?"

"That couple, apparently." Meghan glanced at the TV screen. The cake was a masterpiece or a monstrosity, depending on your point of view. It was certainly big.

"I can't really see the point," Quinn said. "But then I can't see the point of any of it, really."

Ah. So there was the warning. Message received, loud and clear. "No, I can't either, really."

He slid her a smiling but curious glance. "Never wanted the whole white wedding scenario? Cake, dress, the works?"

"Not really." She took a deep breath, decided for honesty. "Actually, I was engaged once."

Quinn raised his eyebrows, clearly surprised and maybe even disconcerted by that little nugget of information. "You were?"

"A long time ago. It didn't work out. Obviously. Which was a good thing." Meghan rose from the sofa. "Do you want a drink? There's some wine left—"

"Do you have anything stronger?"

"Whiskey?" She had a bottle in the back of the cupboard.

Quinn's mouth curved and his eyes gleamed. "Now that's what I'm talking about."

She dug the bottle out of the cupboard and poured two healthy measures. Neither of them was driving; Quinn had walked up from the hotel.

When she returned to the living room he'd turned the TV off and was sitting up a bit more, with one arm resting along the back of the sofa. If Meghan sat on the sofa with him, his fingers might brush her shoulder. She handed him his drink, dithered for a few seconds, and then sat down. What the hell.

His fingers did brush her shoulder, the tiniest of touches that still made longing pulse deep inside her, a jolting sensation that felt like both pleasure and pain. Then he moved his hand away and Meghan sat back on the sofa, acting as if she didn't miss that tiny, brief caress. As if it hadn't affected her way too much.

"So why did you come back?" she asked as she took a sip of the whiskey and let it burn its way down her throat, setting up a mellow fire in her belly. "Really?"

Quinn cocked his head, smiling faintly. "You don't seem to believe me when I say I want to repair the hotel."

"You could have hired people to do that."

"Not on ten grand."

"But why come at all?" she pressed. "Why do you care? Because you didn't when you first came here."

Quinn took a sip of whiskey, his gaze becoming distant. "I didn't know the place. Still don't, not much anyway, but it was my home once, and that means something. And I've seen how much the hotel once meant to the town..." He shrugged. "I want to do what I can." He swiveled so their gazes met, his lips twisting wryly. "I'm a regular Boy Scout."

"People will help you," Meghan said. "Everyone wants to see the hotel back in business."

Quinn's expression turned a little guarded. "There's no guarantee it will remain a hotel."

"Anything's better than nothing." She rotated her glass in her hands, staring down at the amber liquid. "I'll do the patch jobs for free—" she began, but Quinn was already shaking his head.

"No charity, Meghan. I neither need nor want it."

"Fine. You can pay for my materials, but not my labor. You can't afford to get everything done otherwise, Quinn." And she wanted him to get it done. She wanted to see the hotel improved, changed. Hell, the whole town.

"I know I can't." Quinn sighed and leaned back against the sofa. "I wish I could."

"That means a lot to people here."

He lifted his head to give her a narrowed glance. "The place will be sold to the highest bidder, no matter what. That won't change, Meghan."

It felt like another warning. "I know that."

His gaze rested on her thoughtfully, and Meghan felt the tension tauten the air between them. "So the last time I saw you," he said slowly, "you seemed pretty pissed off."

"Did I?" she said as lightly as she could. "Maybe that's

because you propositioned me."

"And that offended you?"

No. "I'd like to be offered more than a hour."

His lips quirked. "But that's all the time you had."

"Even so." She took a large sip of whiskey, needing the alcoholic burn.

"So what more do you want?" Quinn asked after a moment.

Meghan met his gaze, saw the hint of a challenge in his eyes. Felt anticipation lick along her veins, along with no small amount of terror. *What was she doing?* "Are you saying your initial offer is still open?"

Quinn shrugged. "It's always open."

"Sounds like you make that offer to a lot of women."

His gaze was completely unrepentant. "Not at the same time."

Meghan rolled her eyes. "Oh. Well. *That's* a relief."

"Just want to keep things clear."

"Right. Thanks." She stared down at her drink, the welter of emotions a complicated tangle inside her. She was both gratified and alarmed by Quinn's interest. How could the man be nice to Polly and wash her dishes and then make it clear he just wanted a quickie? It wasn't fair.

Quinn leaned forward, resting his hand on her shoulder. The feel of his palm through the thin cotton of her sweater was like a brand, jolting her whole body into hyperawareness. Meghan sucked in a quick, revealing breath. "Does it offend you?" he asked in a low voice. "My... offer?" His hand stayed on her shoulder.

"Why should it offend me that you want to sleep with me?" Meghan returned, trying for flippant. "Most guys will sleep with anything with two X chromosomes, so..."

Something flashed in his eyes, annoyance or maybe even hurt, although surely Quinn Freeman had way too many notches on his bedpost to be insulted by her assessment. Meghan raised her eyebrows. "Does *that* offend you?"

"Maybe a little." He eased back, dropping his hand from her shoulder. "I don't normally consider myself quite such a horn dog."

"Well." Meghan shrugged. "I guess you want a booty call while you're up north."

"That's not what I was suggesting."

"An hour?" She reminded him even as she wondered why she was purposely picking a fight. She'd had a nice time tonight, and she *was* tempted by Quinn's offer. So why act so pissy?

Quinn shook his head, smiling, although Meghan thought underneath all that laidback charm he was more than a little annoyed. "That really got to you, didn't it?"

"It was telling."

"Fine. If you want all night, let's go all night. I'm game." His heated gaze clashed with hers. "What's the holdup? This can be simple. We're attracted to each other..."

"Confident of that, are you?"

"Meghan." Now he sounded genuinely amused. "Do you want me to prove it to you?"

"No." She only just kept herself from scrambling off the sofa. "I just don't like cocky guys."

"Sorry," he said, but he didn't sound remotely contrite. "I thought I was simply stating the obvious." He leaned forward. "On *both* sides. You're the only woman in this town I'd even think of sleeping with."

Was she supposed to say thank you? "Well, you've certainly made yourself clear." Meghan let out a rush of breath. "And I'll admit I'm tempted." She gestured to the house, Polly's bedroom. "You've seen my life. No one's beating down the door with offers like yours. Not tempting ones, anyway." She tried for a smile. "The truth is I don't get out a lot."

"I know." He spoke gently, which made her feel even more twisted up inside. It would have been easier to say yes to sex if she didn't like him as much as she did, but how on earth could she explain that to Quinn?

"I don't know, though," she said slowly. "It seems complicated."

"How so?"

Meghan could hardly believe they were talking about sex like it was some business deal. But maybe to Quinn it was. "This is a small town. If you spent the night here everyone would know it. People are probably already talking—"

"I didn't bring my truck—"

"Planning ahead, were you?" She shook her head, torn between amusement and annoyance. "Someone saw you come in. Someone else would see you leave. Or Polly would say something or someone would see you coming back to the hotel, or *something*. There's always something."

"Fine." He shrugged. "So the whole town knows we had sex. Is that such a big deal?"

She stared at him in disbelief. "Clearly you haven't been in Creighton Falls for that long."

"You know I haven't."

"Yes, it would be a big deal. It would be in the *Watertown Daily News*, with accompanying pictures."

His mouth curved. "Having sex is front page news in upstate New York?"

"Having sex with a Freeman. Yes."

"Ah." Quinn's gaze shuttered and he looked away. "Is that what this is about?"

"That you're a Freeman? It's a big deal, whether you realize it or not. Whether you like it or not." Suddenly the sex issue seemed bizarrely secondary. Quinn was still looking away. "Do you like being a Freeman?" she asked. "Here, I mean? Do you mind that everyone knows you, remembers you?"

Quinn shifted in his seat. "Not really." He glanced back at her, and Meghan had the sense that a mask had dropped into place. "As the youngest Freeman brother, I'm used to being known. I've always been Adam or Jake's kid brother."

"To whom?"

"To everyone we knew. School, especially. We all went to the same boys' boarding school." He smiled, his his voice light. "Too bad I wasn't as academically minded as they were."

She wasn't really surprised, but she still wondered. "Why not?"

"Never saw the point."

"Did you go to college?"

"Dropped out senior year. Didn't see the point of that, either."

And yet he'd completed three years of college? There had to be something Quinn wasn't saying, but Meghan had no idea what it was.

"It's getting late," Quinn said, and put his unfinished whiskey on the side table with a decisive clink. "I should probably go."

"So I guess I can't take you up on your offer tonight?" Meghan dared to tease, and Quinn gave her a sudden, scorching look.

"Were you intending to?"

"I…" Meghan stuttered, alarmed and excited by the blatant male heat she saw in Quinn's eyes, as well as the answering leap of desire she felt in her belly. "No," she admitted, and he rose from the sofa.

"Let me know if you change your mind."

Would she? For a second Meghan pictured it. Naked

bodies, blazing kisses, hands on skin. Heat crawled its way up her neck, bloomed in her cheeks. Quinn took a step closer to her.

"You're picturing it, aren't you? Right now?" he murmured. "You're definitely thinking about it."

"I wouldn't be human if I wasn't," Meghan retorted. Quinn smiled.

"Good," he said, and before she knew what he was doing, he took another step toward her, leaned down, and brushed his mouth against hers. A kiss. It was a kiss, so quick and shocking that her senses short-circuited. She hadn't been kissed on the mouth in ten years. Not that Quinn ever needed to know that. "Bye, Meghan," he murmured, his lips hovering over hers, and then he stepped away. In the next moment he was gone, walking down her front path, a gust of cold air blowing the door closed before he'd reached the gate.

Chapter Nine

QUINN SPENT THE next week working hard, sweating out his sexual frustration. Kissing Meghan had been a mistake. Hell, maybe going to her house, spending time with her at all, had been a mistake. It had made him want her all the more, and right now she was off-limits by her own decree. Quinn thought he could change her mind if he put some effort into it, but the truth was he wasn't sure he wanted to. He wanted Meghan, no question about that, but she'd been right when she'd said it was complicated. Every day he spent in Creighton Falls made him realize how complicated it was.

This town *expected* things of him, and he wasn't used to that. They looked at him like he was a hero in the making, and he damn well knew he wasn't. Tossing out a bunch of moldy furniture and replacing some floorboards didn't make him a saint. The hotel was still going to be sold, no question. But the people of Creighton Falls had hope, and that was a dangerous thing.

He'd seen it when he'd gone to the diner for breakfast, and Brenda had given him the calorie-laden Creighton Falls'

Special, three fried eggs and half a pound of bacon with hash browns piled on top, on the house. He'd seen it when people whose names he didn't know had stopped by his booth and asked him how the work on the hotel was going. When Quinn had mentioned the need for a dumpster, he'd found one in the parking lot the next day. Meghan had been right; people wanted to help. They wanted to help him, to follow where he led, and Quinn didn't know what to do with that. He was a screw-up, always had been. Eventually the good people of Creighton Falls would figure that out.

And as far as Meghan went… he didn't want to mess that up. No-strings sex was how he'd always operated but if Meghan wasn't up for it he'd just end up hurting her, and considering her life, that was something he definitely did not want to have happen. Better to walk away from her, keep his distance if he could. He hadn't seen her since they'd had dinner at her house, and that had to be a good thing—even if it didn't feel like it.

"Quinn?" The musical, female voice that floated through the downstairs had Quinn tensing.

"Just a sec," he called as he reached for his shirt, rubbed his face with it and then, with a grimace, yanked it on. "There aren't any floorboards in the hall," he called. "I'll come to you." He made his way back to the kitchen, skirting the gaping holes in the floor, to find Hannah Taylor standing in the doorway, a casserole in her hands.

"Hey, it's good to see you again," she said with a wide

smile.

Quinn nodded his greeting; he hadn't seen Hannah since she'd made it her business to invite him to the talent show three weeks ago.

Now he noticed the flash of the wedding ring as she proffered the covered dish, and wondered what she was up to. A few women had stopped by with casseroles in the last week, and he'd seen the hope in their eyes and felt like fresh bait. Meghan O'Reilly was still the only woman in Creighton Falls he wanted to be with. "Lasagna," Hannah said. "I hope you like it."

"Love it, thanks." It was his third lasagna that week.

"Where shall I put it...?"

"I'll take it." He reached for the dish, noticing the way she was checking him out. Hopefully it was just neighborly curiosity. With her red hair, dark blue eyes, and slender figure, Hannah Taylor was a beautiful woman, but Quinn didn't go for married chicks.

"You've done a lot with the place," she said in approval.

"Emptied it out, mostly."

"Still, it looks a lot better."

"That's good." He smiled at her, willing her to go, because small talk had become hard in this town. He, the natural charmer and easy flatterer, found it hard to make chitchat with people who cared too much. Because it made him start to care, and that was something he wasn't ready to do.

"I was wondering if you were free this weekend?" Hannah asked. "My husband, Sam, and I are tapping trees and we like to have people over, make a party of it. If you'd like that?"

He stared at her blankly. "Tapping trees?"

"To make maple syrup. Kind of a thing around here." She gave him a teasing smile. "I didn't have the first clue until last year. I'm new here."

"Yeah, I think Meghan mentioned that." Hannah's eyes widened and Quinn mentally slapped himself. He'd just added fodder to the town's relentlessly churning gossip mill. "Awhile ago," he added, as if that made it any better.

"Well, we'd love for you to come help us tap a few trees. There's food and beer involved, and you can meet some locals."

He hesitated, because he already felt pretty tangled up with this town. And yet what was the harm? Meghan might not be there and even if she was he could keep his hands off her. And there was beer. "Okay, thanks, I will," Quinn said, and he knew it wasn't the promise of beer that was making him accept.

MEGHAN TURNED INTO Sam Taylor's drive, parking behind a truck that was as mud-splattered as her own. That was spring in upstate New York for you, but despite the rivers of mud, Meghan was grateful for the hint of warmth in the air, the glinting promise of the river.

Next to her, Polly clambered out of her seat, excited to see Hannah and Sam and especially their Black Lab puppy, Daisy.

Meghan followed behind, breathing in the fresh air and enjoying the blue skies and fragile sunlight. It felt good to get out, to be somewhere other than under a sink or elbow-deep in a toilet tank.

"Hey, glad you made it." Hannah appeared at the doorway, a pot of beef stew in her hands. "I'm just bringing the food up to the sugar shack. We can keep it warm up there."

"Can I help?" Meghan asked. Polly was already inside, sprawled on the floor with Daisy, who was excitedly licking her face.

"Sure. Grab the bread rolls. Quinn's already brought up the beer."

"Quinn?" Meghan froze midway to the kitchen. "You invited Quinn Freeman?"

Hannah shrugged, all deliberate nonchalance. "Why not? He's here for a few weeks, maybe even longer. I thought he'd enjoy it."

Meghan's eyes narrowed in suspicion. "Did you invite anyone else?"

Hannah busied herself grabbing napkins and paper plates. "Fiona Denham, but she's visiting her sister in Troy this weekend. And the Slaters, but their kids are sick. I wanted to invite the woman who just bought the general store, Beth somebody, but she's out of town." Hannah blinked at her, baby-eyed.

"Uh-huh."

"What?"

"Everyone else you decided to invite just happened to be unavailable?"

"People are busy. And I'm being neighborly."

"Some would call it interfering."

"Not in Creighton Falls."

Meghan sighed and grabbed the bag of bread rolls. "Fine," she said in dismissal. If she made too big a deal over Quinn being here, Hannah would get even more ideas than she already had.

Hannah grabbed the rest of the food and Meghan called to her sister. Polly came running, the puppy squirming in her arms.

"We're going up to the sugar shack, Poll," Meghan said, and her sister nodded, happy as long as she had the puppy.

They headed outside, picking their way through the muddy yard to the rough track that led through the trees up the hill to a stand of maples where Sam did his sugaring.

"What a glorious day," Hannah said, tilting her head to the sun. "You can almost believe it will warm up."

"Eventually," Meghan agreed with a laugh. Her gaze had arrowed on the familiar figure at the top of the trail. Quinn was dressed in a red plaid flannel shirt, jeans, and battered work boots, which was pretty much what every man in a fifty-mile radius wore, but he looked a hell of a lot better in those clothes than they did. With his muscled physique and blond-streaked hair, he looked like he'd walked right out of an Abercrombie ad. Meghan could feel her heart rate starting to speed up.

Quinn turned as they approached, and even though his expression didn't change, Meghan could tell he hadn't known she'd been going to be there. She felt an awareness leap inside her, almost as if she was connected to him. Could feel his response, or maybe that was just her overwhelming response to him. Her lips tingled even though it had been over a week since he'd kissed her. And such a little kiss it had been, even if she'd felt it in every fiber of her yearning body.

"Hey, Polly." Quinn rescued Daisy from Polly's tight grasp, and the puppy scampered about their feet. "It's good to see you."

"Hi, Quinn, it's good to see you, too," Polly said dutifully—it had taken Meghan months to coach her sister in basic pleasantries—and then she was back looking for the dog.

Quinn turned to Meghan. "Hey." She couldn't tell anything from his face, his friendly yet somehow distant smile. Was he regretting his blatant invitation of a week ago? Maybe he'd taken up a better offer. Not that she'd been obsessing about it or his kiss all week. Not at all.

"Hey," she said, and looked away. She felt as if she was in junior high. Hannah was watching them both avidly.

"So how do we actually do this?" Quinn asked her. "The tapping thing? I'm hoping there's an electric drill involved."

"Sorry, we do this the old-fashioned way." Sam Taylor emerged from the sugar shack, a hand drill in his hand. Meghan had always liked Sam; he was ten years older than her but he'd always been a presence in the village, solid, steady, silent. Getting together with Hannah had brought him out a bit more, and it was heartwarming to see how happy he was, especially since his childhood had been even harder than her own. Hannah and Sam were both happy, and if she sometimes felt a needle-prick of envy, Meghan resolutely ignored it.

"We drill a hole, put the spile in, hang the bucket. Pretty easy," Sam said with a smile for Quinn.

Meghan was trying not to look at Quinn, but it was difficult. He looked so *good.* He rocked a flannel shirt like no one else in this town. She watched out of the corner of her eye as he took the drill from Sam and gave the wooden handle a few experimental turns.

"You're going to have to put some muscle into it," Sam said with a laugh, and Quinn caught Meghan's glance, gave her a slow smile. She felt her cheeks start to heat and she looked away.

She was so busy trying to look relaxed and unconcerned that she missed the rest of what Sam was saying, until Quinn turned to her, a drill in hand, eyebrows raised. "Well?"

"Wait... what?"

"Grab that bucket of spiles. We're partners, O'Reilly."

"Partners...?"

"I'll drill while you hold the spile." He nodded towards Sam, who was heading farther up the hill. "He's doing the north side, we'll do the south. Didn't you hear anything Sam said?"

"What about Polly?"

"Hannah's staying in the sugar shack with her. And Daisy of course, who is clearly the star attraction."

Meghan had no doubt Hannah had arranged this all. Sighing, she grabbed the bucket of spiles. "Why can't I drill and you hold the spiles?" she asked as they walked around the sugar shack to the other side of the hill.

Quinn cocked an eyebrow. "Because holding spiles is a girly job."

Meghan stopped, her mouth dropping open in outrage. "That is so—"

"I'm kidding, Meghan. Go ahead and drill if you want. I'd like to see you getting all worked up and sweaty."

"Do you always flirt?" Meghan demanded in a low voice, and Quinn gave her a smiling glance.

"You call that flirting? I haven't even warmed up yet."

Meghan shook her head, both exasperated and charmed. "I suppose you just can't help it," she said. "It's like a form of Tourette's for you."

QUINN LAUGHED, THE sound echoing through the leafless trees. "Yeah," he agreed, "maybe it is."

"Habitual flirting." Meghan's mouth twitched. "Is there

any cure?"

"Are you offering to be my doctor?"

She let out a huff of laughter. "No."

Quinn just smiled. He'd told himself he'd keep his distance from Meghan today, although it was kind of hard when Hannah was not-so-subtly intent on pushing them together. And as for the flirting... maybe he couldn't help it. Trouble was, he *liked* Meghan. He liked her sassy banter and her determined spirit. He even liked her prickly defensiveness and the flash of irritation that lit up her eyes and made them look bluer. He also like looking at her, with her dark hair streaming all tousled down her shoulders, her cheeks berry-red, and her legs looking endless in a pair of skinny jeans and hiking boots.

"So you want to drill first?" he asked as they came to the first of Sam's sugar maples, marked with a stripe of red paint.

Meghan put down the bucket of spiles. "You can do it since it'll make you feel all macho."

"You're all heart," Quinn answered, and surveyed the tree in front of them, Sam's instructions running through his head.

"Do you actually know what you're doing?" Meghan asked. She sounded like she didn't think he did.

"I've never tapped a tree before, if that's what you're asking," Quinn answered. "I've tapped other things, though." Meghan rolled her eyes. Quinn grinned. "Sorry, I couldn't resist."

"I know."

He really should stop flirting with her. Trouble was, it was so much fun. "Can't be too hard, right?" He glanced at her; her eyes were narrowed, her hands on her hips. "Have you tapped a tree before?"

"No."

"I thought you would have tapped your first tree when you were three or something."

"We never had any sugar maples," Meghan answered. "My dad was a fishing man."

Was? Quinn recalled she'd mentioned a mother who wasn't around and a father who wasn't much use. He wondered about the details now, but knew better than to ask. He didn't really need to involve himself more in Meghan's life. They'd keep to banter. Maybe a little light flirting would satisfy this craving he had to feel his hands on her skin, his mouth—

And maybe not. Quinn shifted where he stood and nodded toward the tree.

"Sam said to drill a hole on the sunny side of the tree, about three feet from the ground. I think I can manage that." He sized up the tree and then put the drill's bit to the bark as he turned the crank. The drill bit through the top layer of bark and then stopped. Meghan let out a soft huff, the sound of skepticism, the soundtrack to his life. Quinn gritted his teeth. Suddenly it felt really, really important to drill this damn tree.

He put his arm into it, and then his whole body, so the bit sank into the tree and the bark floated down in delicate spirals.

"Whoa, Nelly," Meghan murmured, and Quinn realized he might have drilled a little too deep. So maybe he was trying to prove something.

"That should do it," he said, and stepped back. Meghan gave him a knowing look, and Quinn shrugged.

"You were the one who suggested I needed to feel macho."

She shook her head and reached in the bucket for a spile and hook. "And now for the girly job."

Quinn watched as she cleaned the turnings out of the hole and threaded the spile through the hook's eye as neatly as if she were threading a needle. *Definitely* a girl's job. As if he'd said the words aloud, she gave him a reproving glance. Quinn laughed aloud. He'd never had so much fun with a woman before, and they weren't even having sex.

Yet.

He considered the dilemma he found himself in, and wondered again just what he was going to do about it. Perhaps a fling with Meghan O'Reilly didn't *have* to be complicated. And sex with someone he actually liked might be worth experiencing.

Meghan swore under her breath and Quinn's gaze flicked to the tree. She'd cut her thumb on the sharp edge of the spile and as Quinn watched, she put it in her mouth and sucked. He nearly groaned aloud. Did she realize what that did to him?

"Did your hurt yourself?" he asked, his voice coming out a little hoarse.

"Just a cut."

"Let me see." He took her hand, tugging off his own glove so he could examine her thumb more closely. And she let him, as if he had an MD degree, or maybe she was hoping he'd kiss it better. Because that was definitely what he wanted to do.

"It's just a cut," Meghan said again, but now she sounded breathless. Quinn kept his gaze on the droplets of blood welling on her pale skin. The urge to touch her skin to his lips was almost overwhelming.

Then Meghan tugged her hand from his. "Quinn…" she began, and he made the mistake of looking into her eyes. So much need and want in those baby blues. Quinn sucked in a hard breath and then he reached for her.

She didn't resist; his lips crashed down on hers and her mouth opened under his. He backed her up against the tree, one knee wedging between her legs, his hands sliding under her sweater, finding warm, sweet skin.

Meghan gasped aloud. "Your hands are *cold.*"

"Sorry," he muttered against her mouth, but he didn't mean it. Already he was sliding his hand higher, finding the ripe curve of her breast, his thumb flicking over her taut nipple.

"I'm freezing, you realize," Meghan said on a shudder, and Quinn flicked his thumb again.

"Suuure."

She laughed and buried her head in his neck. Quinn liked the feel of her there. He let out a sudden, surprised laugh. "Did you just... *sniff* me?"

"Maybe," she said, her voice muffled against his throat. His hand was still on her breast. He pressed against her, groaning as her hips arched back against him.

"You're going to kill me."

"No, you're going to kill me." She pushed his hand down, her face flushed as she moved away from him. "Seriously, your hands are cold."

He gazed at her dazed expression, her pursed mouth. Talk about conflicting signals. "Is this really that complicated?" he asked quietly.

She stared at him, confusion shadowing her lovely eyes, turning down that lush mouth. She opened her mouth to speak and then a voice floated up to them.

"Quinn? Meghan? How's it going?" It was Hannah.

"Yes," Meghan said, and pushing him aside, she tugged down her sweater and coat and started back down toward the sugar shack.

CHAPTER TEN

HANNAH EYED MEGHAN speculatively as she came into the sugar shack, her face still flushed, her blood still heated. Goodness, but Quinn Freeman could kiss. And other things. The man was a fast mover, no question. She'd barely had time to register his mouth on hers before his hands had been all over her. And they had felt *good*.

"So, lunch?" Meghan asked brightly. Hannah was stirring the stew set over the woodstove and Polly was sitting on the dirt-packed floor, singing softly to Daisy who had resigned herself to her lap.

Hannah's eyes narrowed. "How many trees have you guys tapped?"

"Um, one?"

"*One?*"

"We're new to this."

"You're a local—"

"We didn't do syrup when I was growing up," Meghan answered with a defensive shrug. She felt as if Quinn's brand was on her, a blazing signal of what she'd been up to.

"Sam's probably tapped twenty," Hannah said, her hands

on her hips.

"Like I said, we're new to this. Be happy for the help. Not," she couldn't keep from adding, "that you invited me here to help."

Hannah looked at her, innocence personified. "Why do you think I invited you?"

Meghan just rolled her eyes. Hannah gave her an abashed grin. "Come on, he's cute."

"Cute? *Cute?* Quinn Freeman is not cute, Hannah."

Hannah's eyes lit up with mischief. "Sexy, then."

"Who's sexy?" Sam's voice rumbled from the doorway and both women stiffened, eyes wide in surprise as they stared at each other.

"You, of course," Hannah said swiftly, but Meghan could tell Sam wasn't fooled. She busied herself retrieving paper plates and napkins, and hoped Quinn was making himself useful, drilling holes far away. God help her if he heard the word sexy. He'd have no problem knowing whom they were talking about.

Hannah gave Sam a quick, placating kiss, and being a man who knew his priorities, he dropped the question and returned the kiss. Meghan kept her eyes on the plates.

Polly looked up from playing with Daisy, her eyes widening as she took in Sam and Hannah. "Ew," she said with deep disgust, and they broke apart, laughing.

"Sorry, Polly," Hannah said with a little smile. "Too much PDA."

Polly wrinkled her nose. "What's PDA?"

"Public displays of affection," Hannah explained.

"Do you mean sex?" Polly asked in her blunt way, and Meghan winced.

"Polly…"

"Yes, that's what we mean," Sam answered easily enough. "But not in the sugar shack with people present."

Polly nodded in understanding. "That's not appropriate behavior," she said, a sentence that Meghan had drilled into her long ago. She was used to her sister's bluntness, but the talk of sex with the memory of Quinn's hands on her body made her break out in an all-over prickly flush.

"I'm going out to tap a few more trees," Sam said. "Call me for lunch?"

"Will do," Hannah promised, and after scooping up a handful of spiles, Sam disappeared outside. Hannah raised her eyebrows at Meghan. "So what was that about?"

"What was what about?"

"You're the color of a cherry tomato."

"It's cold outside."

"Meghan. Seriously. Is something going on between… you know?"

Meghan shot a pointed look at her sister. "Not right now, Hannah."

Hannah grinned in delight. "So something is!"

"No. I mean… no." She shook her head, the tingling excitement that had been coursing through her since Quinn's kiss starting to trickle away. "I don't know."

"That's different than a straight no."

Daisy scampered off Polly's lap and Polly got up to follow the dog outside. "Stay by the sugar shack, Poll," Meghan called, and Polly turned to give her an indignant look.

"I'm not a baby."

"I know." With a defeated sigh, Meghan slumped into the shack's one chair. Now there was nothing to keep Hannah from giving her a grilling. Sure enough, Polly had barely made it through the doorway before Hannah turned on her.

"So something is going on between you and Quinn?"

"Not exactly."

"What does that mean?"

Meghan lifted her head to pin her friend with a pointed look. "Why are you so curious?"

"Because I'm happy and I want the people around me to be happy."

"And you think I can be happy with *Quinn?*" Meghan heard the disbelief in her voice, and so did Hannah, because she gave her a questioning look.

"I don't know the guy well enough to say that definitively, but he seems nice and he's certainly easy on the eyes. Why not have a little fun?"

"Now you're sounding like him."

"Oh, I am, am I?" Hannah looked intrigued.

Meghan decided to 'fess up. Her friend was going to drag

the truth from her eventually anyway. "He asked me to have a—well, a one-night stand, I guess." She made a face and Hannah raised her eyebrows.

"You turned him down, I take it?"

"Yes—but that was before he came back."

"Things have changed?"

Yes, because he kissed me and my lips are still tingling. "I don't know," Meghan said slowly. "Maybe."

Hannah turned to the stove to stir the stew thoughtfully. "Well, you know Sam and I started out as a one-night stand."

"TMI, Hannah."

"That is not TMI. I'm just saying, there are worse things."

"So you, a happily married woman, are advocating for me to have no-strings sex with a stranger? Shall I tell that to your children one day?"

Hannah laughed, the sound both wry and uncertain. "Please don't. I don't know, Meghan. To be honest, I wouldn't normally suggest such a thing. I'm definitely more of a relationship kind of girl, but…"

"But?" Meghan prompted when Hannah, her expression clouded, seemed reluctant to go on.

"But I think you deserve a little happiness," Hannah said quietly. "You've had some tough breaks. Why not snatch a little pleasure while you can? And he *is* hot."

"Yes, he is." Meghan schooled her expression into one of

pleasant neutrality. She didn't want Hannah to see how deep her words cut. *Snatch a little pleasure.* The implication being, naturally, that a little pleasure was all that she could get. But maybe Hannah was talking sense. Why hold out for something that might never happen?

"Let me ask you this," Hannah said. "What's keeping you from it, really?"

Meghan thought of the reasons she'd given Quinn. Because he was a Freeman and the last thing she wanted was the town talking about her. Again. They'd talked when her mom had left for Arizona, and when her dad had gone into rehab. They talked about Polly all the time, none of it mean-spirited, most of it sympathetic. But still, talk. The subject of pity or judgment, it didn't matter which. Meghan didn't like either.

"I don't want to be gossiped about," she told Hannah.

"Sweetie, you can live your life like a nun and you're still going to be gossiped about. That's just Creighton Falls. Nobody means it maliciously. They just care."

"I know, but…" Meghan sighed. It wasn't the gossip that was keeping her from leaping off that ledge with Quinn. It was something else, something more and yet less definable. "There's Polly to consider," she said.

Hannah's mouth twitched. "Polly seems like she knows the facts of life."

"Yes, but she doesn't really understand about relationships. If Quinn became important to her and then left, it would be hard."

"So don't let him become important to her. We're talking a fling, not a commitment, right?"

"That's exactly right."

"Maybe," Hannah suggested quietly, "it's not Polly you're worried about, but yourself."

Meghan's head jerked up at that. "What do you mean?"

"That's how it was for me and Sam. I cared about too much, too quickly. It felt unreasonable and yet also right."

Meghan shook her head. "I don't *care* about *Quinn,*" she said stiffly.

Hannah grinned. "Perfect, then you can have a fling."

HANNAH'S WORDS WERE still rattling around in Meghan's brain as she drove home that evening, Polly humming happily to herself in the passenger's seat.

It had been a pleasant afternoon, all told, a fun afternoon. Quinn had come in for lunch having drilled a respectable twenty-five trees; he'd shaken his head when he'd learned Sam had done double that.

"You'll learn," Sam had said as he clapped him on the shoulder. Quinn had smiled and then pretended to rub his arm as if Sam had hurt him; Meghan had wondered just when Quinn would learn. Everyone knew he wasn't sticking around.

They'd eaten lunch outside, sitting on old tree stumps that Sam intended to split into firewood, paper plates of beef stew on their laps. Quinn had seemed totally at ease, and Meghan wondered how he could seem so relaxed in such an unfamiliar setting; he belonged on a yacht or the ski slopes of Switzerland, not slumming it in the backwoods of upstate New York.

And why wasn't he as affected by their kiss as she was? He'd looked completely relaxed while all afternoon her nerve endings had been feeling as if they were scraped raw. It was a painful feeling, but it made you feel alive.

Just like Quinn's kiss had.

Her hands tightened on the wheel as she remembered that kiss in exquisite detail, as she'd been doing all afternoon. Every time she looked at him, every time he spoke, a shiver of longing had run through her. She'd thought of what Hannah had said, how simple she'd made it seem. Why not grab some happiness? Having a fling with Quinn didn't preclude finding something bigger and better later. It didn't have to be selling out.

And it could feel so very good.

As for her worries about town gossip and the fact that he was a Freeman... Meghan sighed. It was a concern, yes, but the town was going to talk no matter what she did. She might as well have some fun while they were at it.

"Can I have a cheese and pickle sandwich when we get home?" Polly asked, leaning forward in her seat.

"Yes, Poll."

"And a Coke?"

Meghan gave her sister a quick smile. "Yes, Poll."

"And watch *Amazing Wedding Cakes?*"

"Yes."

Polly let out a sigh of contentment and leaned back against the seat. Meghan wished she could be as easily satisfied as her sister.

A couple of hours later Polly was settled in bed and Meghan was prowling the house, restless and uneasy. And burning, because that brief, hot kiss had lit her up inside like a firework, and it wasn't going out anytime soon.

With a gusty sigh Meghan slumped onto the sofa and stared at the blank screen of the TV.

The phone rang, and hope leaped inside her even though she knew Quinn didn't know her phone number. But he could have found out…

"Hello?"

"Hey, pumpkin."

The sound of her father's jovial voice, as always, made Meghan feel a tangle of sorrow and hope. "Hey, Dad."

"I thought maybe you could stop by sometime? It's been awhile, hasn't it?"

"Yes…" She and Polly visited their dad the last Sunday of every month. Meghan unloaded four weeks' worth of food into his freezer and left written instructions about how to reheat the meals-for-one. Then she deep cleaned the bathroom, changed the grimy sheets on his bed, and did a vacuum round the tiny living room. After about two hours

Kevin O'Reilly was always at the end of his resources when it came to dealing with Polly, and so they left, another month gone by.

"We're coming tomorrow, Dad," Meghan said. "Like we always do, remember?"

"Oh." Her father sounded as if this was a change in plans. "Right."

"I'll bring some meals."

"You don't have to…" Her father trailed off half-heartedly, and Meghan didn't bother replying. She always brought meals. If she didn't, her father would live on beer and cold cereal, or forget to eat at all.

"Maybe we can go to a game sometime," her father suggested. "The Watertown Bucks are starting preseason…"

"Are they?" Meghan kept her tone noncommittal. Her father was often suggesting they do things together; he never followed through.

"You both all right, though?" Meghan heard a thread of desperation, of loneliness, in his voice now that made her close her eyes.

"Yeah, Dad, we're all right."

"And Polly—"

"She's fine."

Her father sighed, a long, low release of breath that could have meant anything. Satisfaction, sadness, disappointment, regret. Meghan had never been able to tell how much her father felt, whether he regretted ambling away from them both when they'd needed him most.

"Okay, then," he finally said. "See you Saturday."

"See you Saturday," Meghan echoed, and then she hung up the phone.

She sat there for a few more minutes, staring into space, when a knock sounded on the door. A light yet purposeful knock, three brief, hard taps. And Meghan knew bone-deep who it was.

A smile was already spreading across her face as she walked to the door, her whole body starting to tingle. She put her hand on the knob of the front door, the metal cool under the heat of her palm. She waited a few seconds, deliberating whether she wanted to do this. Then she realized there was no question, and she opened the door and stared straight into Quinn's smiling face.

CHAPTER ELEVEN

ALL AFTERNOON QUINN had been debating whether to see Meghan again. Whether to go for it. He'd tried to talk sense to his libido but that didn't seem to work, and then he'd ripped up all the floorboards in the bar room and that didn't work either. He still felt as if he were on fire.

So then he'd decided to stop being such a damned Boy Scout and he drove to the Stop and Shop and bought a bottle of half-decent champagne and two plastic flutes along with a pack of condoms, and then he drove to Meghan's house.

Now he held the bottle of champagne aloft, gave her a playful smile. "I thought you might be up for a drink."

She had a look of blazing determination on her face, and for a second Quinn thought she was going to plant her hands on his chest and push him away so he'd fall flat on his ass, but she didn't. She grabbed fistfuls of his shirt and hauled him toward her instead.

He nearly dropped the bottle of champagne as Meghan's mouth crashed down on his. Somehow he managed to steady them both, fling the bottle of champagne onto a side table, and keep kissing her. That was the most important part.

"I thought you didn't want gossip," he muttered against her lips as he kicked the door closed behind him.

"I don't care anymore," she said breathlessly, and then she kissed him again.

Quinn decided not to ask any more questions. He'd been spending too much time second-guessing both his own intentions and Meghan's. Now he just wanted to act. And so, it seemed, did Meghan.

Her lips remained on his as he backed her into the living room until the back of her knees hit the sofa and she fell onto it, taking him with her.

Quinn threw out an arm to keep from crushing her underneath him but Meghan didn't seem either to notice or to care. She wriggled beneath him and it took Quinn a few seconds to realize she was already taking off her clothes.

"Whoa. Whoa." He stilled her hand with his own. "That hour thing? We don't have to take it so seriously."

She gazed up at him, panting with exertion, her face flushed, her sweater rucked halfway up her chest. Quinn could see the hint of a lace bra and he felt sweat break out on his forehead.

"Don't you want to do this?" Meghan demanded.

"Hell, yes," Quinn answered with feeling. "But it doesn't need to be a sprint."

"Maybe I feel like sprinting," Meghan retorted, and starting tugging his shirt from his shoulders.

"Maybe I don't," Quinn answered, and then wondered why he was protesting so much. Let the lady have her way, by all means. He could sprint if she wanted to.

Meghan had worked her hands under his shirt and was sliding them up his bare chest, a sigh of pleasure escaping her. "How did you get so ripped, pretty boy?" she murmured, and Quinn let out a choked laugh.

"At least now I know what you think of me."

"I think you're incredibly sexy," Meghan told him as she pulled his shirt over his head. It got stuck and Quinn yanked it off impatiently eager for Meghan's hands to be on him again. "And incredibly jacked. Do you lift weights or something?"

"Sometimes. Do you want to know my exercise regime?"

"No, I just want to feel the results." She bent her head and pressed a kiss to his pec. "And taste them."

Quinn let out a groan. "Can we at least go to the bedroom? I haven't had sex on a sofa since I was seventeen."

"Picky," she muttered, but she was smiling, and Quinn felt that last little bit of trepidation he'd been holding melt away. This was going to be okay. This was going to be great. Meghan got it; she understood the rules. It didn't have to be complicated at all.

MEGHAN SASHAYED INTO the bedroom, trying to cling to the determination that was deserting her all too fast. She didn't regret asking Quinn in; she didn't even regret hauling him in by his shirt and basically attacking the man.

But she realized she didn't know how to act now; she had zero experience with one-night stands or no-emotion flings. And Quinn obviously had had plenty, and from a young age at that.

She hadn't tidied her bedroom or even made the bed, and she quickly kicked a bra and pair of underpants into the corner as Quinn came into the room behind her. He put his hands on her shoulders and she let out a little helpless moan as he pressed a kiss to the curve of her neck. He slid his hands down to cup her breasts, his thumbs teasing her nipples before dropping them lower and under her shirt.

One little touch and Meghan felt herself turning liquid. Maybe it didn't matter that she wasn't all that experienced; she'd let Quinn take the lead. She sagged against him, reveling in the feel of his hard, muscled chest against her back, his hands on her skin. Deftly he slipped her shirt up and over her head—he was a sight more accomplished at that task than she had been—and then he popped the button on her jeans and slid a hand down the front.

Meghan let out a quick, sharp gasp at the feel of his searching fingers. He pressed against her experimentally and yet with so much expert knowledge, and she nearly came apart under his hands. She grabbed his wrist, her nails digging into his skin.

"Don't," she managed, and Quinn stilled his hand.

"Don't…?"

"Don't stop," she clarified. She couldn't believe how close to the edge she was already, too close to want to come back so much as a millimeter. "Don't stop," she said again, rocking her hips, and with a low, knowing chuckle Quinn slid one finger underneath her underwear and stroked the damp folds of her sex.

Meghan clenched her teeth, although why she was fighting it she had no idea. It was just so *intense.* Another stroke and then he slipped a finger inside. That was her undoing. She cried aloud, grabbing his hand as she rocked against him and felt her climax crash over her.

She was still shuddering in its aftermath, sagging against him, when Quinn spun her around, pressing her against him, his palms molding to her butt. "Now I call that a good beginning."

Meghan felt as if she could slide into a puddle on the floor. She let out a shaky laugh. "It's been awhile."

"You don't say," Quinn murmured and if she'd had more energy she would have been embarrassed. As it was, she already felt the need pooling once more in her belly. She could feel Quinn's erection straining against his jeans and with a playful smile she rubbed a hand down its impressive length. "So now it's your turn?"

"This is all good," he assured her. "Trust me, it's an incredible turn-on to have a woman come apart so fast and hard." He tugged down her jeans. "I want to see if I can make it happen again."

"You'll kill me."

"But you'll die happy," Quinn murmured, and he helped her to step out of her jeans.

Somehow she was naked. Meghan wasn't quite sure how it happened, but she supposed Quinn was pretty deft in taking off a bra. And then he was naked too; she pulled his jeans down and he kicked them off, and the boxers followed quickly.

She stared at him, reveling in how absolutely *hot* he was, all golden, sculpted muscle, even as she felt a little flicker of trepidation. She'd never done anything like this before.

"I hope you brought a condom."

"Didn't I tell you I was a Boy Scout?" Quinn answered lazily. "But we don't have to jump to the condom stage just yet. There are plenty of things I want to do with you, no condom necessary." And gently, smiling as he did it, he pushed her back onto the bed.

Meghan fell onto the rumpled duvet, gazing up at him in expectation and excitement and just a little bit of alarm. Quinn gave her a wolfish smile and then stretched out on top of her; every point of his body that connected with her own felt like an electrical charge. Meghan couldn't keep herself from arching into him, legs wrapping around his, hips lifted in anticipation.

"Don't jump the gun now," Quinn murmured, and moved his head to her breasts. Meghan's head fell back as he lavished his attention on each one in turn, taking his time, licking and kissing and sucking. Her fingers tangled in his hair as she anchored him to her, craving more and more.

And he gave more and more, moving down her body, kissing and touching every last little bit. Meghan would have felt self-conscious if she hadn't been half out of her mind with need. If Quinn's mouth and tongue and hands weren't driving her right to the edge.

But she wanted to touch him too, she realized through the haze of her own desire, and somehow she summoned the strength to push him onto his back. He rolled over, eyebrows raised, faint smile curving that lovely, mobile mouth. "You can't have all the fun," she said and his mouth curved a little more.

"I think you were having some fun there."

She definitely had been. "You know what I mean," she said and rolled herself on top of him. She'd wanted to touch him, but now that she had Quinn underneath her, ready and waiting, she felt shy. He must have been with a million women. Sexy, experienced women, women who were miles above her in looks and moves.

"Meghan," Quinn said softly. "You could do anything to me and I'd love it. Within reason," he amended hastily. "I know how tough you can be."

She laughed softly and pressed a kiss to his chest. "All right, I guess I won't take the nipple clamps out just now."

"Let's save those for another day."

She laughed again, her breath fanning his bare skin, and

pressed another experimental kiss to his chest. His skin was smooth and hot and his chest hair tickled her cheek. Another kiss, and another, and her mouth hovered around his belly. She could feel his muscles tensing, and she ran a hand along his abdomen.

"Impressive six pack you've got there."

"I try."

She moved her hand lower, letting her fingers slide along his silky length. Quinn's breath hissed through his teeth. Meghan felt a surge of both excitement and power. He liked her touching him. He really did. She slid her hand up and down, ran her thumb gently along the head. And then she chickened out, because as intoxicating and amazing as this all was, she was still somewhat of a novice in the bedroom. A few fumbled experiences with her former fiancé ten years ago didn't really count for much.

She moved back up to kiss his chest and his throat and take a big sniff of his neck. "You smell good," she murmured and Quinn moved so she was half-under him.

"Maybe now it's time for a condom," he suggested, and Meghan was more than ready.

Quinn grabbed one from the back pocket of his jeans that had been kicked onto the floor, and then seconds later he was poised above her and Meghan's breath hitched in her chest. She was ready, she knew she was, and yet it felt so intense, so *emotional,* to be here like this, with Quinn above her, about to join his body with hers.

He slid in slowly and Meghan blinked, adjusting to the size of him, to the feeling of being invaded, overwhelmed.

"Okay?" he murmured and silently she nodded; she didn't think she had the words to describe how she was feeling. Quinn braced himself on his forearms as he began to move, a slow, building rhythm that Meghan started to match. She arched her hips up, meeting his thrusts, feeling the pleasure and intensity start to build. Quinn buried his face in her neck as his body pumped into hers and she knew he was holding himself back, waiting for her to come before he did. And that knowledge was the catalyst that had her spinning over the edge, and she cried out as her body clenched around his and she felt Quinn shudder into her.

Seconds or maybe minutes later he eased back, smiling wryly, and Meghan managed a shaky smile back. She felt, quite suddenly, as if she could burst into tears, and she didn't want Quinn to realize. That would go over well. Not.

Thankfully he rolled over to dispose of the condom, and gave her a couple of seconds to brush at her eyes, take a deep breath, and will the emotion back. She didn't even know why she'd felt it. She knew what this was. She'd gone into it with her eyes wide open.

Quinn rolled onto his back, adjusting the pillow under his head, and Meghan wondered what she was supposed to do now.

"Thanks," she said, and Quinn shot her an amused look.

"Anytime."

"Sorry, this is kind of new to me," Meghan said, and she saw a wariness enter Quinn's eyes before he smiled and said,

"So what does a woman like you do for sex in this town?"

"Learn to be independent?" Meghan suggested with a cocked eyebrow, and Quinn grinned.

"Beyond that."

Meghan shrugged. "Not much, to be honest. I haven't..." She decided not to finish that sentence. Quinn didn't need to know she hadn't had sex in ten years. Not since Ben.

"Which makes me wonder why you didn't take me up on my offer instantly," Quinn murmured.

"Don't start getting arrogant," Meghan warned him. "Because no matter how ripped you are, that is seriously a turn-off."

"Noted."

She hesitated, wondering if she should get off the bed, get dressed, show him the door. Quinn must have sensed her uncertainty because he reached out an arm and wrapped it around her shoulders.

"It hasn't even been an hour," he murmured, and pulled her to him.

Meghan went awkwardly, but as her head hit his shoulder her body seemed to know what to do, fitting itself against his. She breathed him in and closed her eyes, let herself enjoy this moment. Because that was all this was, all she had. A moment.

QUINN STROKED MEGHAN'S bare shoulder as he felt her relax into him. He was surprised at how much he enjoyed the simple feel of her against him. Usually he was pretty quick to be on his way after sex. The women he'd chosen as bed partners had never been ones he'd been keen to cuddle or do the whole pillow talk thing with. Meghan was different.

But not that different. She'd understood his rules. She knew this was a fling. Except, for a few seconds there, she'd looked as if she'd been about to cry. Quinn wasn't sure if he'd been imagining that moment of emotion; he hoped he had. God knew he didn't think he could handle it. But he wasn't quite ready to make his exit yet.

Seemed like Meghan was, though. She stirred in his arms even though she'd only been there for a few minutes. Her hair brushed against his chest and Quinn tightened his grip, tried to keep her in place. He might as well have been hanging onto a fish. Meghan slipped away from him and Quinn watched her go, admiring her lithe, naked form even as he felt a flicker of irritation or maybe even hurt that she'd left him so easily. *He* was the one who left.

"What's up?" he asked lightly and she didn't look at him as she reached for her jeans.

"It's late."

Quinn glanced at the clock. "It's nine-thirty."

Meghan just shrugged, her hair flying about her face. In the dim room, the only light coming from the half-open door, Quinn couldn't see her face.

"I thought you wanted more than an hour," he teased, but that joke was getting old and Meghan was pulling on her shirt. In a few minutes he was going to be kicked out, and wasn't that a new experience. Not one he really wanted to try, actually. Quinn swung his legs over the edge of the bed. He took his time getting dressed, letting his gaze rove over her room, curious now about Meghan's personal space, about Meghan herself.

He saw a thick, academic-looking book on her nightstand, next to a bedside lamp that was decorated in a pattern of blue and green mosaics. Meghan caught his stare and he gestured to it. "Nice."

"Thanks." She was pulling her hair into a ponytail, and it felt like reassembling her armor. Quinn was still naked.

He reached for the book, raising his eyebrows at the title. "*A Thousand Years in the History of Art?*"

She snatched the book from him, tossing it onto a pile of folded clothes. "I like history."

"Interesting." He wondered why she was so touchy, and then he wondered why he was making small talk. Why not just beat it? They were done here.

"So." She folded her arms, gave him a challenging look, chin lifted, mouth pursed.

Quinn leaned back against the pillows. "Are you showing

me the door?" he asked, trying to sound amused rather than annoyed as he felt.

"I didn't think you'd want to spoon."

No, he surely didn't. So why was he hanging around? His gaze swept over her, noticing the tightly folded arms, as if she were trying to keep herself together. "You seem spooked."

"No." She spoke quickly, meeting his gaze. "But it's late and I've got to work tomorrow."

"Okay." Trying to stay relaxed, not to betray his irritation, Quinn unfolded himself from her bed. He stretched, and watched her appreciative gaze slide down his body. He knew he could convince her to let him stay. He was pretty sure if he so much as touched her she'd melt. Again.

But what was the point? They'd both gotten what they wanted here, and he'd never been one to stick around. It still didn't feel good, though, having her watch him dress as if she couldn't wait until he was gone. Not good at all.

He took his time buttoning his jeans, pulling on his shirt, and all the while Meghan stood and watched him, her arms folded, one foot starting to tap.

"I'm starting to feel like I couldn't get out of here fast enough."

Her eyes widened as she took his meaning. "It's not that... I'm not that..."

Quinn held up a hand to stop her stammering. "It's okay, Meghan. I'm not looking to stay the night." Although he sort of had been, weirdly enough.

"I've never done this before," she said in a rush. "I don't know the protocol."

He stopped, one hand still on the button of his jeans. "You've had sex before, though."

"Yes, but not… not *this*." She gestured to the rumpled bed. "I know what this is, Quinn. You don't need to worry that I'm going to get notions. I signed up for no-strings sex and that's what I want. My life's too complicated to have someone like you in it."

He decided to let the *someone like you* comment pass. "Okay…"

"It's just I don't know how to handle these awkward moments. So forgive me if I seem a little abrupt." Her voice came out with an edge, and he saw a defensive glitter in her eyes. Meghan O'Reilly was a whole handful of contradictions. Tough and tender all at once, sassy and vulnerable. Too much for him to take.

"You're handling them fine," he said. "I'll go." But first he pulled her toward him, because he wanted to touch her one more time. She resisted at first, coming slowly, until he tugged a little harder and their hips bumped and she let out a breathy little sigh. Quinn ran a thumb over her soft, kiss-swollen lips before framing her face with his hands. Her skin was petal-soft, although the hands that came up to grab fistfuls of his shirt were callused from work.

"Are you sure you want me to go?" he murmured.

"It's better this way. Polly…"

Quinn nodded. "Okay," he said, and brushed a goodbye kiss across her lips. "I'll see you Monday."

"Monday…" One kiss and Meghan sounded dazed.

"If you have time, you can start work on the plumbing of the hotel. Or if not, you could just stop by and say hello." He brushed another kiss across her lips and then, because that just wasn't enough, he went deeper, sweeping his tongue into her mouth, tasting her softness.

Meghan sagged beneath his hands, her body going soft and pliant against his. Then she straightened and with effort pushed away from him.

Quinn watched her in regret. He could have definitely kept going, but it was better this way.

"Monday," he said, a promise, and then he walked out of the bedroom. Seemed they both needed reminding of his rules.

Chapter Twelve

"SO THAT SHOULD keep you for a couple of weeks."

Meghan closed the freezer and turned to her father with a determined smile. He stood in the center of his tiny kitchen, shoulders slumped, hands in the pockets of his too baggy jeans.

"Thanks, sweetheart. You're good to me."

"It's not a problem, Dad." Meghan reached for a bottle of cleaning spray and a cloth. Time to blitz the house.

Her father watched her as she sprayed all the kitchen surfaces, wiping them briskly as she moved around him.

"You okay, love bug?" he asked.

"Fine, never better." She scrubbed at a hardened stain on the counter; hopefully it was ketchup and not blood.

"You seem a little… tense."

"I'm not tense," she said, although actually she was. She'd been tense all day, her body buzzing with the aftershocks of Quinn's lovemaking last night, her mind seething with questions and doubts. Polly had, as she often did, picked up on her mood, and been more challenging than usual. It had been a pitched battle to get her sister's hair brushed and face washed.

"Work okay?" Kevin asked, and Meghan sighed.

"Yeah, work is fine." Her father tried as best he could, he really did, but it wasn't the same. She'd been taking care of him since she was sixteen, when her mother had left and her father had, at her urging, finally checked himself into rehab. Twelve years later he was sober and mostly solvent, and that was about all.

"Polly...?" Kevin tried, hesitantly, because Meghan suspected he knew how he'd let them both down when it came to Polly.

"She's fine." She was watching a show on Meghan's phone in the living room, but Meghan suspected her sister would get bored soon. She had to keep these visits tight. "Sorry, Dad," she said as she moved around him to get to the sink. The drain was clogged with soggy Cheerios. "I just need to get this clean."

Her father smiled tiredly as he stepped toward the door. "I'll move out of your way."

Two hours later the house was clean and Meghan was saying goodbye, giving her father a hug as she chivvied Polly out the door.

"The Bucks are playing next weekend," her dad said as Meghan reached for the handle of the front door. "I thought I'd get some tickets."

"Yeah, sounds good," Meghan agreed. Her dad couldn't afford the tickets, and Polly wouldn't sit still for the game, but it would never happen anyway. It never did.

"See you next month," Meghan said, not even pretending now that things were different, and then she was gone.

Twenty-four hours later she was pulling into the parking lot of the hotel, her heart going like a jackhammer. What exactly did Quinn expect today? What did she want? She'd spent the last two days going over Quinn's words again and again, picking apart their meaning, his tone, his look.

At least she'd managed to avoid Hannah and anyone else in Creighton Falls who was inclined to give her a grilling. And since no one had sought her out, Meghan thought she might have actually gotten away with it. No one knew what was going on between her and Quinn, so why shouldn't she just enjoy it? Ride this train until the last stop?

Taking a deep breath, Meghan got out of her truck. She heard the sound of hammering as soon as she stepped through the back door. The place was already starting to look better, she noticed as she walked through the swept-clean kitchen and into the back hallway. The moldy wallpaper had been stripped from the walls, and Meghan edged around gaping holes in the floor where the rotten boards had been removed.

She found Quinn in the front hallway, laying down fresh floor boards. She took a moment to admire his physique, bronzed muscle gleaming with healthy male sweat. He was wearing nothing but a pair of jeans and work boots, and Meghan didn't think she'd seen a finer sight in her life.

She took the opportunity to speak when he stopped hammering for a second. "You've been busy."

He turned, startled, but his surprise morphed into a knowing grin as his gaze heated and swept over her. "I have."

He made everything sound like a sexual innuendo. Already Meghan could feel herself starting to warm. To want. "I came here to start some of the plumbing work," she said, although that wasn't totally true. She'd come because she wanted to see him. Touch him.

"Damn, and I was hoping you'd come for sex."

She laughed, grateful for his bluntness and daring to match it. "That, too."

He rose in one fluid movement, muscles rippling. Meghan swallowed hard. "I'm very glad to hear it."

"But first let me at least start on the repair work," Meghan said. He was walking toward her with loose-limbed confidence and it made her nervous. She still couldn't completely enter into the spirit of the thing. The fling.

"By all means," Quinn said as he reached for her. "But first let me say hello."

His hello was a deep, endless kiss that had Meghan grabbing onto slick muscle to keep herself upright.

"*That* was hello?" she managed when Quinn finally eased back.

"Mmm-hmm." He looked like he was going in for a second greeting and it took all of Meghan's willpower to pull away.

"Let me do my work," she said, and swatted him on the arm. He just grinned.

She went through the hotel again, more slowly this time, including the upstairs; Quinn had repaired the stairs, stripping the carpets and ripping up and replacing old floorboards.

The place had a feeling of energy and optimism now that the rot and mold had been cleared away, although upstairs Meghan saw that not much had been changed yet. She walked through the sixteen elegantly proportioned bedrooms, all of them with ensuites, focusing on the plumbing and yet conscious of the feeling that everything had been forgotten, lost. Some of the rooms still had furniture; all of them had their old fixtures, silk-striped wallpaper, an aura of melancholy that Meghan could feel settling on herself.

She stood in the center of one of the bedrooms, gazing out at the town green; the snow had finally melted and the crocuses and daffodils were peeking out of flowerbeds. The town's center had the same air of forlorn neglect as the hotel, with half the stores shuttered and the playground equipment and bandstand needing repair. For one blazing second Meghan longed to see her hometown fresh and vital again, just as the hotel was becoming.

But only to be sold. In a few weeks Quinn would finish here, return to New York or go on to Thailand or Bali or wherever next he felt like traveling. The world was open to him, every last bit of it, and his stint in Creighton Falls was nothing but a short detour. And she was part of that.

It was nothing Meghan hadn't told herself before, and yet she kept on needing the reminder. *This wasn't permanent. Don't get attached. People leave.* They left Creighton Falls and they left her. Time and time again.

"Hey." Quinn's voice was low and husky, and the floorboards creaked as he came toward her. "What are you doing?"

"Staring into space. Wasting time."

"And billing me for it?" he teased, and she turned to him with a smile.

"I told you I wouldn't charge you for labor."

He stood in front of her, his gaze searching her face. "You had another look at the plumbing?"

"Yes." She gestured to the clipboard she was holding. "With the other work I already have scheduled, I can probably get it done within two weeks. Just patch jobs to see you through."

"Okay." He stood before her, gazing at her steadily, a half-smile on his face although his forehead was furrowed.

"What?" she said. "You look… funny."

"You look sad."

Surprised, she shook her head. "No."

He cradled her cheek with his palm, a touch so gentle she felt tears prick her eyes. So much for not seeming sad. "You sure?"

"Yes." This wasn't part of their deal, was it? Quinn

wasn't supposed to be all touchy-feely like this. She didn't understand why he was, but she knew part of her yearned for it. Longed to have someone she could unburden herself to, lean on, trust. Too bad that wasn't Quinn.

"So, my work here is done for today." She needed to get back for Polly's return.

Quinn's thoughtful smile turned wicked. "Then it's time for play," he said, and reached for her.

Meghan didn't resist. Hadn't she wanted this from the moment she'd walked through the door? From the moment he'd left her house two days ago. This part was easy. He slid his hands up to cradle her face as his lips tasted hers, but already it wasn't enough. Already she was opening her mouth, kissing him hungrily, needing more.

The moment's tenderness turned urgent, raw, as Quinn deepened his kiss, his hands sliding down to tug at her shirt. He backed her up to the window and hoisted her up effortlessly to rest her bottom on the sill. Meghan wrapped her legs around his hips as he pressed into her. She could feel his fingers fumbling with the button on her jeans and she laughed breathlessly.

"The entire town of Creighton Falls will be able to see my backside if they look up."

"No one's looking up."

"Still..." She didn't offer any more resistance because Quinn had found his way into her jeans, and his fingers were stroking her with such deft surety that she couldn't think at all. So what if the entire town saw? In that moment she didn't care. In that moment all she wanted was Quinn, and she wanted it wild and fast and hard. She needed the oblivion, a moment's escape from the reality of her life.

"Of course you have a condom," she muttered as he slid one out of his back pocket.

"Are you kidding? I've been carrying one of these since I met you."

"I bet you've been carrying one of those since you were twelve," Meghan returned but right then she didn't care about how many women Quinn had had, or how experienced they'd been. All that mattered was that he was with her now, that he'd chosen her *now*.

And then he was inside her, filling her up, hot and hard and deep, and she wrapped her legs even more tightly around his hips as she brought him closer, her face buried in his shoulder as she matched him thrust for thrust.

The windowsill groaned and the glass at her back creaked and in a distant, fogged part of her brain Meghan realized there was a distinct possibility of falling out the window, through the porch roof, and landing half-naked onto the sidewalk below. Then she decided it was worth the risk.

Definitely worth the risk, she acknowledged moments later, with her climax still shuddering through her and Quinn resting his forehead against hers.

"Now we've really given Creighton Falls something to talk about."

She let out a ragged laugh. "Don't. I can't believe I've showed my butt to the entire town."

He peered over her shoulder. "No one's looking. No one except Billy Kargas, anyway."

"What!" Meghan started to scramble away from the sill but laughing, Quinn held her tight. "I'm only kidding." She relaxed against him until he added, "It's just Brenda Wickley."

"Nice try." She wouldn't be fooled a second time. "She isn't out there really, is she?" she couldn't keep from asking and Quinn stroked the hair from her face, tucking it gently behind her ears.

"No one's out there, Meghan."

"Good." She wriggled, felt him groan a bit as he already started to harden again inside her. "I should move, though," she said. "This glass is kind of cold."

"You're always complaining about the cold." Reluctantly Quinn pulled away from her, disposing of the condom and pulling up his jeans. Meghan cleaned herself up, conscious of that weird tangle of feelings—a boneless sense of pleasure and an even deeper happiness, and over it all an unease she couldn't quite articulate even to herself.

"I should go…"

"First let me show you the work I've done," Quinn said and surprised, Meghan let him tug her by the hand and lead her downstairs.

They went through the downstairs rooms slowly, with

Quinn describing the furniture he'd thrown out, the few pieces he was having restored, the floorboards he'd repaired, the wallpaper he'd stripped.

"It's just general clean up work," he said, but Meghan knew he was quietly proud, and she was proud of him. He hadn't had to come back up here, do this all himself. He could have walked away from Creighton Falls like everyone else in his family had.

"You've done a lot in a couple of weeks."

Quinn shrugged off her praise even though he was smiling. "Nothing too taxing, but it feels good to see the place starting to come back to life. This building has good bones."

"It does, doesn't it?" They were standing in the huge sitting room, the wood-paneled walls and ornate fireplace giving the room a haunting sense of its former glory. "Has being here helped you to remember anything?" Meghan asked. "About the past? Your past, I mean? Living here?"

Quinn's gaze shuttered and he shook his head. "Not really." He jammed his hands in the pockets of his jeans. "A little bit," he admitted, the words drawn from him reluctantly. "I remember having a Christmas tree in here. And... bringing it in with my dad. He patted my head. In a nice way, I mean. It was... it was a good memory." He went quiet, and Meghan felt her heart turn over. The moment he'd described was so small and fleeting, and yet so poignant.

"I'm sorry, Quinn."

He glanced at her, one eyebrow arched, not quite able to

recapture his usually insouciant self. "What for?"

"For losing your father that way. For growing up without him. It must have been incredibly hard."

Quinn shrugged. "It was for everyone else, but I was young enough not to understand what was going on. And I've never really known anything else."

"Still, you lost your father, a crucial person in your life." Her voice thickened as she thought of how she had, in a different way, lost hers. "Nothing prepares you for that."

Quinn's gaze retrained on her, and Meghan knew he'd heard the emotion in her voice. "And you seem to have lost both your parents, even though they're still alive."

"Yeah. Well." How had they started having such a deep conversation? And *why?* Meghan glanced at the lengthening shadows of twilight outside and stirred herself. "I should go. Polly will be home soon." She glanced at her watch, and sucked in a hard breath. "Damn, she's probably already home." With nobody waiting for her. Polly didn't handle change in routine, especially unexpected change, well.

"And you need to be there?" Quinn asked, his voice sharpening with realization.

"I always need to be there." Meghan started striding toward the kitchen door, where she'd dumped her coat. She skirted the gaping holes in the floor, Quinn following her.

She'd left her phone in her coat pocket and she swore aloud as she looked at its glowing screen. Five missed calls from Betty.

Quinn came to stand beside her, one hand on her shoulder. "Is everything okay?"

"No, Betty..." Meghan shook her head impatiently, not having time to explain it. She pressed redial and a few seconds later Betty answered her phone. "Betty—"

"I'm sorry, Meghan, but I had to leave her at your place. I've got Debbie at work tonight, and I'm watching the twins..."

"I know. I'm sorry I wasn't there." Betty had a daughter who was a single mom and she ended up providing most of the childcare. Taking Polly to and from work on top of that was an act of generosity on her part.

"She was a bit upset that you weren't there," Betty admitted. "But she got inside okay and I had to leave..."

"It's okay, Betty. It's not your fault." A heaviness settled inside her. "It's mine."

As soon as she'd disconnected the call, she was grabbing her coat, heading for the door.

"Wait," Quinn said, reaching for her. Meghan shrugged him off. "What's going on?"

"Betty dropped Polly off at home," she explained tightly. She could feel a burning in her chest, a wave of panic rising inside her. "And I wasn't there."

Quinn didn't say anything for a second, and Meghan was glad he didn't ask the expected question. *And that's bad? You have to be there?*

Yes, she damn well did. She wrenched open the door.

"Wait, Meghan—"

"I can't wait. Polly might be upset, agitated—"

"Let me come with you."

She jerked around to stare at him in surprise. "What—"

"Just in case," Quinn said, and Meghan didn't dare ask in case of what. She realized she wanted someone there; she wanted Quinn there. Wordlessly she nodded, and Quinn followed her out to her truck.

Five minutes later they were parked in front of the ramshackle ranch house she called home. Meghan yanked the keys out of the ignition and sprinted inside.

"Polly?" she called but she'd known the moment she'd opened the door that Polly wasn't there. She felt the emptiness reverberate through her. "Polly," she called again, her voice pleading, as if Polly might come out of hiding. It only took a few seconds to go through the house: kitchen, living room, two small bedrooms.

Quinn had followed her into the house, and now stood in the living room, watching her.

Meghan took a deep breath in an attempt to stave off the encroaching panic. She still heard it in her voice, felt it in her hammering heart, her clenched fists. "Quinn," she said, and she sounded like a child asking for help. "She's not here."

CHAPTER THIRTEEN

Q UINN SAW THE naked fear on Meghan's face and he felt
like he'd do anything to make it go away. He reached a
hand out to her and she jerked away, even though he hadn't
touched her.

"What do you want me to do?" he asked, but it was as if
she hadn't heard him.

She turned away from him, pressing one fist hard to her
forehead. "I should have been here. I'm *always* here. And
Polly doesn't do change." She took a gulping, shuddering
breath. "She could be anywhere. Who knows what she was
thinking or feeling…"

"Then let's go find her," Quinn said steadily. "I'll drive
and you can look."

"What if she's not on a road?" Meghan demanded, her
voice high and shrill. "What if she's in the woods or by the
river…" She stopped abruptly, biting her lip, and Quinn felt
his stomach muscles clench.

The river. Bad things happened at the river. *On* the river.
He knew the ice had melted, although great chunks of it still
churned in the dark water. Would Polly be tempted to go

there, by herself, in the dark? He didn't think so, but he didn't really know Polly or understand how her mind worked.

"Let's think logically," he said, keeping his voice calm. "Where do you think she would go?"

"I don't *know*—" Meghan closed her eyes briefly. "It depends on what her mood was like. If she was angry with me not being at home, she might go off into the woods in a temper. But if she was scared or sad..." Her voice hitched and Quinn ached to take her into his arms. The urge surprised him, strong as it was. He didn't do that sort of thing. He didn't like emotion; no one in his family did. It was messy, complicated, painful. But right now he wanted to make Meghan feel better. That was paramount, along with finding Polly.

"This is totally my fault," she said, her voice ragged with self-recrimination. "I should have been here. *I should have been here.*"

"Blaming yourself now won't do any good right now, Meghan," Quinn said. "Why don't we divide and conquer? I'll look in the woods and you can drive around town."

"You don't know the woods. I'll go there and you can drive." Meghan's tortured gaze met his fleetingly before she looked away.

"Okay. We'll do that. You have your phone?"

"Yes, but the cell reception is patchy, especially in the woods."

"Take it anyway. I have mine."

"I don't actually have your number—"

"Here." Quinn took her phone and programmed his number into it, and then sent a text from her phone to his. He'd rather stay with her, make sure she was okay along with Polly, but he knew Meghan needed to act. He handed her back her phone and then took her by the shoulders, needing to touch her, to comfort her as best as he could. "It's going to be all right."

He didn't miss the flash of anger that lit her eyes before she twisted away from him. "You can't say that," she said. "You don't know that. How could you possibly know that?"

Quinn blinked, forcing down the affront—no, the hurt—he felt at her words. She was upset and angry with herself. He couldn't take what she said at face value.

"Maybe not," he agreed calmly. "But panicking won't help Polly."

She bit her lip, and then with a jerky nod she tossed him her car keys. "Use my truck. Polly will recognize it, if you see her. I'll go look in the woods." And she turned and walked out of the house.

Quinn took a measured breath. It was true, he didn't know that things were going to be okay. Still, he wanted her to trust him, to lean on him, and she wasn't having it. Could he really blame her? No one had leaned on him, ever. But right now he wished one woman would.

He trawled the few streets of Creighton Falls slowly,

hunched over the wheel, peering into the darkness. The village green was empty, the gazebo abandoned. He stopped the truck in front of the diner and had a look through the fogged windows at the handful of people occupying the vinyl booths, but he couldn't see Polly. He thought about alerting people to the fact that she was missing, but he suspected Meghan wouldn't want everyone in her business. She'd barely wanted to involve him.

He checked his phone repeatedly, but had nothing from Meghan. Reception was patchy anywhere in the town, so he couldn't even be sure he'd get a text or call anyway. Fifteen minutes had passed and he was starting to feel antsy, wondering if they should call the police. He couldn't suppress a creeping alarm, a choking sense of fear; he couldn't remember feeling it before and yet it was eerily familiar. That blank place in his mind was starting to fill with shadowy, time-misted shapes.

He turned down the road out of town that led to the defunct marina and a couple of old farmhouses, including Sam and Hannah's. And he slammed on the brakes when he saw a figure huddled by the side of the road, knees drawn to chest as she rocked.

"Polly." He was halfway out of the truck, his voice loud and harsh in the silence of the cold night, when he realized he needed to calm down. He closed the door carefully, gave Meghan's sister a reassuring smile. "Hey. Remember me? Quinn?"

Tears streaked Polly's face and she was trembling with cold. "Yes…" Her voice wobbled uncertainly.

"What are you doing out here all by yourself?"

"I wanted to find Daisy, but it's so *dark…*"

Of course. Polly had been near-obsessed with Sam and Hannah's puppy last weekend. "Meghan's looking for you. Do you want to get in the truck and I'll take you to her?"

Polly bit her lip, her round-eyed gaze moving from Quinn to the truck. "Meghan always says I shouldn't get in cars with strangers."

"That's right. But this is Meghan's truck, and I'm not exactly a stranger, am I?"

"No…" Polly started to rock back and forth again, her arms still wrapped around her shivering body. She let out a choked sob. "I want Meghan. I want *Meghan.*"

"Of course you do." Compassion twisted hard inside him; Polly had clearly reached the end of her fragile resources. "Meghan wants to see you, Polly," he said. "She's waiting for you." He had one wavering bar of reception on his phone, and he pressed Meghan's number, praying the call would go through.

"Quinn?" Meghan's voice faded in and out amidst static but she managed to hear his response.

"I've found her."

"Oh thank God—"

"Here she is." He handed the phone to Polly, who let out another sob as she clutched at the phone.

"Meghan—"

"Polly, go with Quinn, okay? I'm waiting at home. Go with him—" The connection crackled and went dead. Polly stared at Quinn.

"See?" he said encouragingly. "I'll take you to Meghan."

He took the phone from Polly and then put one hand carefully on her shoulder. "Come get in the truck, Polly, and I'll take you right to her, promise."

Polly nodded jerkily and Quinn started to guide her toward the truck. She didn't resist, and slowly he managed to get her in, buckled into the passenger seat. He hopped in the driver's side and turned the truck around before driving back to Meghan's house.

Meghan was wrenching the door from the hinges before he'd come to a stop. She ran around to the passenger side and yanked open the door, letting out a sob as she put her arms around Polly.

"Meghan, I couldn't find you," Polly exclaimed tearfully, and then buried her head in her sister's shoulder.

"I'm sorry, Polly. I'm so, so sorry." Meghan stroked her sister's hair, her arms tight around her.

Quinn got out of the truck. "Why don't we go inside," he suggested, and wordlessly, her arms still around her sister, Meghan guided them both inside. Quinn closed the door of the truck and followed.

He wanted to make himself useful, but Meghan wasn't even looking at him as she bustled around, getting a sandwich and Coke for Polly and turning on *Amazing Wedding Cakes*, clearly the comfort drill. Quinn waited, wanting to help, and it took him a few minutes to realize Meghan actually was angry, and maybe even with him.

She ushered him into the kitchen when Polly was settled in front of the TV and then stood there like a school matron, arms folded, chin held high. "Thank you," she said stiffly. "For finding her."

"I'm just glad I did." Quinn looked at her closely, trying to figure out where the anger was coming from. "What's going on, Meghan?" he asked quietly.

She shook her head, biting her lip, and for a second Quinn didn't think she was going to say anything. "I should have been here," she finally said, her voice cracking. "If anything had happened…"

"But nothing did."

"It doesn't matter," Meghan answered with a vehement shake of her head. "I shouldn't have been away from home." She raised eyes full of both resentment and tears. "I shouldn't have been with you."

Ah. So that's what it was. He'd distracted her from being a saint. "You're allowed to have a life, Meghan."

"Says who?"

"The important thing is nothing bad happened and you *were* here, in the end. Don't beat yourself up over this, Meghan."

"You don't understand—"

"I know I don't," Quinn answered evenly. "But I want to. I want to help."

"Why—" she demanded, the word torn from her, and damned if he had an answer. He could see she was struggling with tears and this time they didn't alarm him. He did the only thing he felt he could do, the thing that felt so natural and completely right. He hugged her.

Meghan's body went rigid with shock and for a few seconds Quinn felt like he was hugging a block of wood. Then she melted into his embrace, wrapping her arms around him as she pressed her face into his shoulder. Her body shook with the force of her emotion and Quinn realizing she was crying. Sobbing, actually, and it was okay. He stroked her back and whispered soothing nonsense and after a few minutes she pushed herself away from him, scrubbing her face with her hands. "I need to deal with Polly."

"I'll be here."

"It might be awhile—"

"I'll wait."

She nodded, her hands still covering her face, and then she dropped them and without looking at him left the room.

WHAT WAS HAPPENING? Every emotion, every fear and need and hope, felt too close to the surface as Meghan went back into the living room and sat next to Polly. She put her arm around her sister and pressed her face, still wet with tears, against her hair. She couldn't remember the last time she'd cried like that. Certainly not since she'd been a child. She'd probably completely freaked Quinn out, except... he hadn't seemed freaked out. He'd been patient and kind and so wonderfully understanding, even though she still struggled with an irrational anger that this was at least in part his fault. If he hadn't been in her life, if he wasn't such a delicious distraction...

But no, she couldn't really blame Quinn. The only person to blame was herself, for being distracted, for putting Polly second. For risking her sister's life. Meghan let out a shuddering breath and tightened her grip on Polly's shoulder.

"Ouch, too tight," Polly complained, and she relaxed a little.

"Sorry, Poll."

She could hear Quinn moving about in the kitchen and wondered what he was doing. Wondered, too, how long he would wait, and what would happen after Polly went to bed. Was he expecting another booty call? She was way too drained, and even though part of her resisted the idea, she figured she should end things with Quinn tonight. There wasn't room in her life for Polly and a relationship, even a no-strings fling one. There just wasn't.

She watched the rest of *Amazing Wedding Cakes* with Polly, all the while wondering what Quinn was up to. Maybe he was just avoiding an awkward scene. After the episode was over, Meghan helped Polly to get ready for bed even though it wasn't that late. Her sister was completely exhausted.

"I'm glad Quinn found me," Polly said once she was snuggled in bed, Meghan perched on its edge.

"So am I, Poll."

"Where were you?" There was no accusation in her sister's voice, just curiosity, and yet Meghan still felt a hot rush of guilt. And of something else, as she remembered that afternoon with Quinn. The desperate urgency she'd felt, along with the pleasure and the happiness. Well, she'd snatched her moment, and now it was over.

"I got caught up at work."

"Caught up?" Polly wrinkled her nose. "Who was catching you?"

"Sorry, it's just an expression." Polly always took things literally. "I was busy and I didn't realize how late it was, that's all."

"Quinn's nice, though, isn't he?"

So already her sister was becoming attached. *Just as she was.* "Yes, Polly, he's nice. But he's leaving soon."

"Where is he going?"

"Home."

"But this is home."

Smiling sadly, Meghan shook her head. She didn't think she was up for an explanation right then, and thankfully Polly was too sleepy to demand one. A few minutes later her sister's eyelids were fluttering and Meghan slipped out of her room. Time to face Quinn.

She came into the kitchen, stopping short when she saw the table laid for two, and several pots bubbling on the stove.

"What…"

"I hope you don't mind. I thought you'd be hungry."

She was hungry, and she was also dumbfounded. Quinn had *cooked* for her? "Thank you," she managed. "It smells delicious."

"Just basic pasta." He'd managed to take the few wilting vegetables from her fridge and turn them into a primavera sauce, which was more than she did most nights.

"It looks and smells amazing."

"Shall we eat?" Quinn started to ladle the pasta and sauce onto two plates while Meghan stood there, physically exhausted, emotionally spent, and wondering just what was going on. He'd magicked a bottle of white wine from somewhere—Meghan certainly hadn't had one in the cupboard—and poured them both glasses.

"Thank you," Meghan said. Quinn put his hand on her shoulders and guided her to a kitchen chair. She slumped into it, accepting the glass of wine Quinn pressed into her hand. Tears pricked her eyes. She couldn't believe she had any left. "Why are you being so nice to me?"

"All I did was make dinner."

"Still." She took a sip of wine, not sure whether she wanted to press the point. Maybe she should take this kindness at face value. Except she'd decided to end it with Quinn tonight. Yet how could she do that when he'd held her as she'd cried and made her dinner afterward?

Quinn sat across from her, smiling, looking relaxed. "Dig in," he said, and Meghan picked up her fork.

The pasta was simple but delicious, and tasted even better for someone else having made it. "I can't remember the last time someone cooked for me," Meghan said.

Quinn cocked his head. "Sounds like it's about time."

Meghan took a deep breath. "Quinn…" she began, although she didn't know how to finish it. How did you end a fling? *It was fun but…?* Shouldn't that have been his line?

"Tell me about Polly," Quinn said, and Meghan's breath leaked from her lungs.

"What…?"

"Tell me about her," he repeated quietly. "Why are you her sole caretaker? What are her issues? How do you cope?" He leaned back in his seat, smiling faintly although his eyes were serious. "Tell me, Meghan. I want to know."

"Why?" she burst out. "We're just…"

"Friends," he inserted firmly. "We can be friends, can't we?"

"I don't know. This wasn't… what I expected."

"Me neither, and yet here we are." He paused, his expression turning wary. "Do you… want to tell me?" he asked, and for the first time he sounded uncertain. Vulnerable.

And Meghan realized she did want to tell him. A lot. She wanted to talk to someone honestly and openly, someone who listened and cared. And amazingly, right now that person was Quinn.

She took a deep breath and nodded slowly. "Okay," she said, and Quinn settled back in his seat to listen.

CHAPTER FOURTEEN

IF QUINN COULD have predicted the events of the evening, they wouldn't have looked anything like this. After Meghan had left the hotel, he would have done some more work, fixing the floorboards in the hall maybe, and then he would have cracked open a beer, ordered a pizza and spent the evening relaxing.

Yet here he was, drinking wine and eating a meal he'd made himself and listening to a woman he realized he was actually starting to care about.

Except he wasn't going to think too hard about that just now. Now he was going to listen.

"I think we realized something was going on with Polly when she was around three," Meghan said. She spoke slowly, choosing her words with care as she rotated her wine glass between her slender fingers, her gaze distant, her dark hair falling forward to brush her cheek. Quinn suppressed the urge to tuck it behind her ear, let his fingers skim her cheek. One touch and he'd be lost. Hell, so would she.

"No one could really put a finger on it," Meghan said as she glanced up at him. "Not me, and not my mother or father. She was just... different." She paused, lost in memory, and Quinn waited for her to gather her thoughts. "She was late talking," Meghan said after a moment. "And when she did talk... well, you know how she is now. She just responded to everything differently than most people. And she had massive triggers, things that set her off screaming or hurting herself—that was awful. She used to lie down and bang her head against the floor. She always had a big bruise right here." Meghan gestured to her forehead. "We've worked on the triggers a lot since she was little, and her coping strategies are much better, but she couldn't stand any loud noises or change in her routine. She still eats the same thing for dinner every night." The smile she gave him was fleeting and sad and just about broke his heart.

"A cheese and pickle sandwich and a Coke?"

"How did you notice that?" He shrugged and Meghan shook her head, almost angry. "It would be easier if you weren't interested, you know. If you didn't *care.*"

"Easier how?"

"To say goodbye in a couple of weeks." She drew a quick breath. "How much longer till you've done what you've needed with the hotel, Quinn? A week? Two?"

"I still have the electrics to think of," Quinn said. He knew he wasn't answering her question but the truth was he didn't how to. He didn't know what he wanted from Meghan, or what exactly was going on here. He was, he realized, breaking his own rules. "You still have a lot of pipes to patch," he reminded her. "Anyway, we were talking about Polly. What happened to your parents?"

"I thought you said we were talking about Polly."

"Your parents are part of that picture. Or they were. Why aren't they now?"

She let out a long sigh. "They haven't been involved for about ten years."

"Why not?"

She lifted one shoulder in a careless shrug, but he could see how tightly she clenched her wineglass. "My dad's always been… carefree. Like a child, almost, although in a different way from Polly. He ran a fishing boat for tourists before the hotel closed, and he loved it, but he was never big into responsibility. Basic things just didn't cross his mind. Paying bills or dealing with life's to-do list. It was okay while my mom was around. She worked as a nurse in Watertown and she was the opposite of my dad."

"Was…?"

"Is. She's still alive. She lives out in Arizona with her second husband, Tony." Meghan grimaced.

"Not a fan?" Quinn asked lightly.

"Nope. But anyway when we were growing up… she did her best by Polly, initially. She took her to a raft of child psychologists and therapists to try to get a diagnosis, but nothing seemed to fit. They ended up slapping the PDD label on her, which felt like they were giving up."

"PDD?" It was a term Quinn had never heard before.

"Pervasive Developmental Disorder. It's a genuine thing, a group of disorders characterized by delays in development of social and communication skills."

"Sounds like you're reeling that off by heart."

"Yeah." Meghan smiled wryly. "I've said it enough, through the years. The trouble is, there's a huge spectrum within PDD. People who can barely function on their own and people like Polly, who can hold down a job and manage for themselves a bit."

"But Polly can't really manage by herself, can she?" Quinn said gently. "She couldn't handle coming home alone tonight."

"I know. And that might be my fault. I should help her become more independent, but it's so tiring and time consuming. Sometimes it's just easier to do it all myself."

"Until you burn out."

"Hasn't happened yet." She gave him a smile that didn't reach her eyes and twirled some spaghetti around her fork. "This really is delicious," she said as she popped the forkful of pasta into her mouth.

"So your mom and dad," Quinn said after a moment. He loved watching Meghan eat, loved watching her do just about anything, but he wouldn't be distracted now. "What happened there?"

"Mom couldn't cope with Dad and Polly, basically. Dad was unemployed and drinking too much. Polly was... Polly. And Polly at twelve was harder than Polly at twenty-four believe me. She'd have a meltdown just about every day. Sometimes she'd scratch or bite you. She couldn't help it," she added defensively, and Quinn nodded.

"I know."

Meghan sighed and slumped in her seat. "At the beginning of eleventh grade, my mom announced she was leaving. She'd met Tony, a businessman from Albany who had been visiting his stepdaughter at the hospital where Mom worked. He was moving to Arizona, and my mom decided to go with him."

It sounded pretty damn heartless to Quinn. "And what about you and Polly? How old was she then?"

"Twelve, and I was sixteen. My mom invited us to come to Arizona with her, after she and Tony were settled." She grimaced. "We flew out the following summer, and it was awful. They had this McMansion with white everything and these two little toy dogs that they called their *children.*" Meghan's voice choked and she shook her head angrily. "Her babies. She didn't even seem to realize how offensive that was. How hurtful." She took a deep breath, willing the emotion back although her eyes remained bright. "And Polly picked up on the tension. It was already hard for her—flying, living in a strange house… we were way out of her comfort zone, and she didn't cope well with any of it. We left after two weeks. I quit school and got the plumbing apprenticeship, and my dad went into rehab." She stopped, as if that was the end of the story, instead of its awful beginning.

"That all sounds really tough," Quinn said quietly. The words were heartfelt but they still didn't feel like enough.

"It was what it was."

"Which was tough."

"Yeah." She cracked a small smile and took another sip of wine. "Yeah. It was." She stared down into her wine, and Quinn felt like she'd admitted something big. Something obvious, at least to him, but important to Meghan. Maybe she'd never been able to say that before. Maybe there had been no one to say it to.

"So your dad was in rehab…?" he prompted gently when she seemed disinclined to say anything more.

Meghan sighed and put down her glass. "He stayed in for three months and then he got an apartment halfway to Watertown and picked up what work he could, mostly highway construction when it happened. There was never any question of him coming to live with us, helping to take care of Polly. He wasn't up for it. He could barely take care of himself."

Quinn glanced around the room. "So this is the house you grew up in?"

"No, we lost that when I was a teenager. This is the house I rented when Dad went into rehab." She grimaced. "Sorry. It's a sad, depressing little story."

"Don't be sorry. It's not your fault."

"Even so. Who wants to hear about someone's dysfunctional family?"

Quinn gave her the ghost of a smile. "If you want to talk about dysfunctional…"

Meghan smiled sadly. "You guys seemed like the fairy tale when I was growing up. But I guess that changed when your dad died."

"Yeah." Quinn wished he hadn't mentioned it. He didn't actually want to talk about his family, his father. Not even about the things he couldn't remember.

"Your mother never remarried, I guess?"

"No. I can't even imagine it, to be honest. She's been loyal to my father's memory."

"She must have spoken about him, then. You must have memories of him, through her."

"No." He could feel a familiar tightness in his chest. "Actually, we never talk about my father. It's… it's almost like he never existed."

Meghan frowned. "That's kind of weird."

"I know."

"You never asked?"

"No." How could he explain the hushed silence of his home life, the feeling that to mention his father, the accident, all of it, would be like stepping on thin ice, falling through just as his father had, into the choking black water below?

"Why not?" Meghan asked. Her voice was gentle, her eyes kind. Quinn looked away.

"I never wanted to."

"But…"

"It just felt better not to. I can't explain it better than that." Didn't want to explain that his father's death had been his fault, and he was pretty sure everyone blamed him still. "We should finish this wine." He poured the rest of the bottle out between them. Meghan watching him without speaking.

"Thank you, Quinn," she said quietly. "Thank you for being so kind tonight. You've gone well and beyond the call of duty."

He arched an eyebrow, striving for light. "Duty?"

"Or the constraints of a fling. I don't know. Whatever this is."

And the trouble was, he didn't know what *this* was. It was rapidly becoming something more than just a fling, something more than he'd ever had before. Something important.

"I was happy to," he said, and meant it. "Thank you for telling me about your parents and Polly."

A silence descended that wasn't exactly uncomfortable, but it wasn't great either. It was awkward, because neither of them knew what to do. He'd never been in this situation before. He'd never simply *been* with a woman, wanting to stay, and longer than just for the night.

"I'll do the dishes," Meghan said as she rose from the table. "Since you cooked." Quinn rose, about to protest, but Meghan shooed him away. "Go relax. You deserve it."

Seemed she wanted him to stay too. Smiling, he retreated to the living room. He felt too restless to watch TV, and so he prowled around the room, noticing the homey touches. The sage-green walls, the framed photos of Polly through the years, and one lovely one of Meghan and her sister, arms around each other, faces pressed cheek to cheek. The frames were done in mosaics, the same as her bedside lamp, pretty, intricate patterns of blue and violet and cream.

He inspected the bookshelf full of paperbacks, surprised at how weighty some of the works were. History, politics, art. He was still looking at them when Meghan came into the room, drying her hands on a dish towel before setting it aside.

"You like to read," he said, a statement.

"When I have time."

"How come you didn't go to college?"

"Couldn't."

He straightened, turned to look at her. "Would you have, if you could?"

"Yes." She hesitated. "I wanted to do a degree in art. Talk about most pointless major, ever. Especially up here."

"Not necessarily." Realization dawned. "The mosaics on the frames and lamp. Yours?" She nodded almost shyly. "They're really good."

"Thanks." A pause. "Why did you drop out of college?"

"My brothers are the ones who got the brains." It was his pat answer, needlessly flippant, and Meghan wasn't fooled.

Of course she wasn't. They'd gotten beyond that, for better or for worse.

"You're smart, Quinn."

He shrugged. "It didn't seem worth it, in the end."

"Yet you did three years of college. You must have been almost finished."

He'd forgotten he'd told her he'd dropped out in his final year. A small yet salient detail. "Yeah."

"What was your major?"

"Business."

Her gaze swept over him, slow, thoughtful, thorough. "What was your GPA?"

His lips twitched. "2.0, Miss Detective." He'd wrecked his junior year, after the blow up with Adam. "Sorry, if you're looking for misunderstood genius, you're wasting your time."

"I just want to figure out what you're keeping from me."

"Nothing, really." Nothing important, anyway. He spread his hands, gave her a careless smile. "What you see is what you get. I'm really very shallow."

"Right." She sounded like she didn't believe him. And he could understand why; he could see it all happening in her brain. He'd come back to work on the hotel. He'd asked her about Polly. It wouldn't take much for someone like Meghan, someone who hadn't had a fair deal in life, to start constructing castles in the air. Making him more of a man than he was. And if he had any sense, any sense at all, he'd

put her straight. He'd tell her, no, *show* her, the truth—
before she was disappointed.

Trouble was, he liked the way she looked at him, like he
was somebody she admired and respected. He liked the way
it made him feel, like he really was that man. He could be.

"Hey," he said softly, and reached out to take her hand
and tug her toward him.

A smile curved her lips. "Hey."

He kissed her, brushing his mouth across hers once,
twice, before he stayed his lips on hers, breathing in the scent
and taste of her as satisfaction and contentment settled on
him. "I'm not a hero." Even now he felt compelled to
remind her of the truth, just in case she really was getting
ideas.

"Is that what you're afraid of?" she whispered against his
mouth. "That I'm going to put you up on a pedestal?" Her
lips brushed his; she was toying with him. "I told you I
didn't like cocky guys."

"So you did." He hooked his thumbs in the belt loops of
her jeans. "So you did."

She laughed softly and then she put her arms around
him, and they were back on firm and familiar ground, except
somehow it felt different.

It felt different when Meghan took the lead and tugged
him toward the bedroom, different when she shimmied out
of her clothes and then pushed him gently back on her bed.
Different when she straddled him, smiling faintly, her eyes

bright, her expression bold.

Gone was the woman who had been shy about touching him, who had confessed she didn't know how everything worked. Tonight Meghan was a seductress, confident, sexy, powerful.

"You do have a condom, right?" she asked as she unbuttoned his jeans.

"In my back pocket, same as usual."

She huffed a laugh and shook her head, her smile wicked. "So predictable."

"I'd hate to disappoint." Her hand brushed his erection as she reached for the condom. "Imagine if I didn't have a condom," he said, his voice turning a little ragged, his expression becoming glazed as he watched her tear open the foil packet with her teeth. "Think how disappointing that would be."

"Much better to be predictable," Meghan agreed, and rolled the condom onto him. The breath hissed through his teeth as he arched up instinctively. "Patience, Quinn," Meghan chided, but he knew she was just as affected as he was. She rose up on her knees and then sank slowly on top of him, her gaze widening just as his was as their bodies joined.

Quinn's hands fisted in the sheet as he pumped his hips. "You're gorgeous, Meghan. So gorgeous." She tossed her hair over her shoulders, triumph and desire in her smile, and Quinn couldn't keep from touching her. He grabbed her hips, anchoring her to him as their bodies met in rhythm and rode together toward climax, voices joining in jagged cries as pleasure overwhelmed them.

Afterward Meghan lay with her head on his chest, her hair in a dark cloud about her face, its strands brushing his cheek. Quinn felt as if he could stay like this forever, and wasn't that a strange feeling. Yet good, too. Pretty damn wonderful, actually.

Last time he'd been in Meghan's bed she'd slipped away from him like water cupped in his hands but tonight she didn't. She rested her hand, slender and strong, soft yet callused, over his for a moment. "Stay," she said softly.

Quinn's heart bumped in his chest. One word, so softly spoken, and yet he felt as if it changed everything for him. Or maybe it simply confirmed that everything had already changed.

"Yes," he answered simply, and then he rested his other hand over hers, sealing her hand between his, almost as if he could bind her even more closely to him.

CHAPTER FIFTEEN

H
OW HAD THINGS changed so quickly? It seemed like one day Meghan was keeping Quinn at a distance, trying to keep to their rules, not wanting things to be complicated. And then the next everything suddenly seemed gloriously simple.

He stayed the night, and Meghan slept in his arms. She hadn't realized how wonderful it felt to lie next to someone for a whole eight hours. To tangle legs, to feel the steady thud of a heartbeat against her cheek. To not feel alone.

She feared the morning might be awkward, but it wasn't. While she slept, Quinn got up and made coffee, and when Meghan finally lurched awake, heart thudding because she'd never slept in so late, she stumbled into the kitchen, rubbing sleep from her eyes and her hair sticking up in six directions, to discover Quinn chatting with Polly over their Cheerios.

Polly grinned and waved, clearly delighted to be the subject of Quinn's attention, and Meghan felt a lurching mix of hope and fear, joy and worry. It was so *good* to see Quinn being part of her life that it hurt. And it would hurt even more when he wasn't any longer.

But in that moment, with the sunshine pooling on the floor and Quinn smiling at her, looking so relaxed and easy, Meghan made a conscious decision not to think that way. Not to worry about when Quinn was leaving, or how she was going to get hurt. She'd spent a lot of her life living that way, because so many people had left. Her mother, her father, her fiancé.

Nope, she was going to try something different this time. She was going to live in the moment, live it to the full, and pay the price only when she had to.

"You've got a funny look on your face," Quinn said, and Meghan stepped further into the kitchen, reached for the coffee pot.

"Just hungry," she said lightly. *And happy.* She smiled at Quinn and poured her coffee.

Quinn seemed to have gotten the same memo she had, because Meghan couldn't help but notice that he was acting differently too. No reminders about rules or flings or any of the rest of it, just a kiss goodbye and a promise to see her later, when she came to the hotel to start work on the plumbing repairs.

And later, when she did come to the hotel, he kissed her again. They worked easily together, Meghan doing an epoxy patch on one of the downstairs bathrooms while Quinn stripped wallpaper from the hallway. It helped that he was shirtless. She could always look at Quinn shirtless. And they talked too, not about anything important or emotional, just easy chat. But even that was nice and weirdly new, to talk with a man who'd seen her naked and liked what he saw.

At four o'clock Quinn pulled her away from beneath a sink, kissed her thoroughly, and then murmured against her lips, "You should go in a minute, if you want to be back for Polly."

Meghan stared at him, speechless for a few seconds. Quinn smiled. "What? You're amazed by my sensitivity?"

"Yes," she admitted with a little laugh. "I am."

"Don't be so shocked," he grumbled good-naturedly, and then kissed her again. "Although actually," he admitted, "so am I."

She laughed again, wrapping her arms around him as she returned his kiss—and that was how Hannah found them a few minutes later.

She gave an over-loud clearing of her throat as Meghan and Quinn broke apart, Quinn smiling easily and Meghan feeling her face start to heat. Hannah was grinning.

"So." She planted her hands on her hips and gave them both an inquiring look. Meghan rolled her eyes and Quinn just kept smiling. "I came over to ask Quinn if he wanted to come to the Bingo Night on Tuesday, but maybe you've already extended an invitation?" She arched an eyebrow at Meghan.

"No, I haven't had the chance."

"A Bingo Night? How could I say no?"

"Easily," Meghan muttered.

"Spoilsport. She loves it really," Hannah assured Quinn. "Underneath. And so does Polly."

"So of course she'll go." Quinn turned his smiling gaze on Meghan and she felt a rush of emotion that was too sweet and strong to bear. Quinn understood her so well. How had that happened? Some of the emotion must have been visible on her face because he frowned slightly, a question in his eyes.

"I will go," Meghan said, her voice a little thick. "Polly loves bingo. She's great at remembering numbers."

"Better than faces?" Quinn said with a smile, and Meghan knew he was referencing their first unfortunate meeting that Polly hadn't connected to Quinn.

"Yes," she agreed. "Better than faces."

She ended up walking out with Hannah, which was unavoidable but also awkward, because her friend didn't even wait until Quinn had closed the door before she was grabbing Meghan's arm and squealing.

"You have *so* much to tell me, Meghan O'Reilly!"

"If you think I'm going to spill all the details, you've got another thing coming."

"But you—and Quinn—"

"That one surely isn't too hard to figure out?" Meghan returned dryly. Hannah squealed again.

"I knew something was going on between you two! I could *feel* the chemistry up at the sugar shack."

And so had she. Meghan didn't reply, but nothing would

deter Hannah now. "So? You're having a fling?"

"Looks like it." She kept her voice light, determined not to think through the consequences, the broken heart she'd be piecing together when Quinn left—when? In a week? Two weeks? Maybe three?

"I'm happy for you, Meghan," Hannah said quietly, dropping the squealy excitement for a moment. She laid a hand on Meghan's arm, staying her. "I just don't want to see you get hurt."

"Now you're giving me that advice?" Meghan said with a laugh. "It's a little late."

"Is it?" Hannah's eyes were dark, her expression serious. "Are you falling in love with him?"

"I didn't mean…" Exasperated, Meghan blew out a breath and shook off Hannah's hand. "I'm just going to enjoy what this is for however long it lasts. And I'm not looking to paint rainbows, and I don't want anyone else in this town doing it, either."

"That's a tall order. Everyone in this town is painting rainbows since a Freeman came back." Hannah nodded toward the hotel. "They want to see it open again."

"You know Quinn isn't here to do that," Meghan said, even as she felt an uncomfortable clenching in her belly.

"We all know it. Doesn't keep us from hoping, though. People want to help."

"I know, and Quinn appreciates it." Meghan climbed into her truck. "But he'll be leaving in a few weeks, and there

will be a big 'for sale' sign up there. And I'm okay with that."
She lifted her chin defiantly, but Hannah wasn't fooled. She
just nodded sadly and Meghan started the truck.

QUINN HAD NEVER played bingo before. A gap in his social
education, he realized as he entered the church hall where the
talent show had taken place a month ago. This time long
tables had been set up in the hall, with a table at the front
that held the bingo ball popper. Quinn eyed the whole setup
in curious bemusement before Brenda Wickley grabbed his
arm and led him toward a table where the bingo cards were
for sale.

"Now a big boy like you, you can handle eight cards,"
she said, and before Quinn knew what was happening his
arms were filled with different colored bingo cards, four in a
set.

"Eight? I'm not sure—"

"Now, now, you're not going to be wimpy and just go
with four?" Brenda demanded.

"Since it appears to do so would be an insult to my man-
hood, I guess I'm not," Quinn said. He saw Meghan come in
the hall and felt his heart lift. He hadn't seen her in two days,
and it felt like forever.

Her gaze searched him out and a small, secretive smile
flirted with her lips. Quinn knew she was remembering the
last time they'd seen each other, when she'd come to the
hotel and they'd christened one of the bedrooms. There were

twelve bedrooms in that place, and he liked the thought of christening them all.

He waited for her and Polly to get their cards before joining her, knowing that in doing so he was staking a claim in front of the whole town. And so what if he was? He felt like staking a claim, and he didn't think Meghan had a problem with that anymore. Bedroom trysts aside, they hadn't been nearly as clandestine as they had at the beginning.

"Eight cards?" She arched an eyebrow. "Feeling lucky, big shot?"

"Very lucky," he murmured, his gaze resting meaningfully on hers. Meghan smiled again, a quick, sweet thing, and then she scooped up a couple of dabber pens and headed toward one of the long tables.

"If you're having trouble keeping up, Polly can help you. She's a whiz at this."

A few minutes later the tables were filled and Billy Kargas took his place at the ball popping machine.

"He doesn't sing tonight," Meghan murmured and Quinn flashed her a grin.

"Thank goodness for small mercies."

"Or big ones." She uncapped her pen and Quinn did the same. Felt a bolt of pleasure lance through him as Meghan rested her hand on his thigh under the table. It wasn't a sexual gesture, just a comfortable one, and he liked it like that. "Get your pen out, Freeman," she said, and he realized he'd just been staring at her, feeling happy. "Billy's about to begin."

"Polly doesn't have her pen out."

Meghan flashed him a smile. "Polly doesn't need a pen."

"What…?"

"Watch and learn."

Half an hour later his head was starting to hurt as he tried to keep up with Billy's brisk pace of announcing the numbers and marking them on his eight cards. Polly, to his amazement, didn't use a pen, but kept track of all the numbers in her head.

"Don't mention *Rain Man*," Meghan warned him under her breath, and he nodded in understanding.

"I would never dare to pigeonhole Polly."

"You'd be the first then," Meghan answered, and then shook her head. "Actually, that's not fair. Everyone has been good to her in this town. To us. But it's hard when you're not familiar with Polly's condition not to make stupid assumptions."

"You'll have to tell me when I do, then."

"You haven't yet," Meghan answered. "You're a natural with her."

"Bar our first meeting," Quinn answered wryly, and Meghan laughed.

All in all it was a good evening, the bingo-playing more fun than he expected, along with everyone's banter as Billy called the numbers, the good-natured ribbing and joking that made Quinn smile. Made him feel a part of things, maybe for the first time in his life. Sitting next to Meghan with her hand on his leg had definitely been a highlight of the evening, as well.

When the evening ended, Polly having scooped up twenty bucks in prize money while Quinn and Meghan didn't have any, they all ambled toward the parking lot, comfortable in the knowledge that they were leaving together. Meghan didn't even seem to mind the speculative looks that came their way.

"Come back?" she asked, shooting him a questioning glance, and Quinn nodded. Hell yes, he was coming back.

"Hey Quinn, Meghan," Hannah called. "I wanted to catch you before you both left."

He exchanged a wry look with Meghan as they both waited for Hannah to bustle over.

"Sam's taking the boat out on Saturday and we wondered if you wanted to come." She smiled at Meghan. "I know Polly loves being out on the water."

"She does," Meghan confirmed. "That would be great, Hannah, if…" She glanced at Quinn who managed a stiff smile.

"Yeah. Sounds great." He could feel his stomach clenching at the thought of being out on that river. But he'd been on the water plenty of times before; hell, he'd kayaked down the Amazon and scuba dived on the Great Barrier Reef. He didn't need to be afraid of a little motorboat on the St. Lawrence. Not at all. "Looking forward to it," he added for good measure and Hannah waved goodbye.

He thought he'd been pretty convincing until Meghan asked him about it later, after Polly had gone to bed. She stood in the doorway of the living room, her arms folded, her expression pensive.

"Are you sure about going out on the river?"

"What?" Quinn glanced up from the TV where he'd been watching the highlights of the Yankees' spring training. "Yeah, sure. Why wouldn't I be?" Stupid question. He didn't actually want Meghan answering it.

"Because of the accident. With your father." She came into the room and sat on the edge of the sofa. "We've never really talked about it."

"Because I don't remember." He heard the edge of defensiveness in his voice and wished he could keep himself from it. He didn't want to argue with Meghan, but he didn't want to talk about this either.

Her gaze searched his face. "You really don't remember anything about it?"

"I told you I didn't." Except for that choking sense of panic he'd had when he'd first looked at the damned river. "What is this about, Meghan?"

"You know so much about my life, Quinn. You've helped me with Polly—"

"I like Polly."

Gratitude and some deeper emotion flashed in her eyes. "I guess I just want to reciprocate a little."

"It doesn't have to work that way. This isn't tit for tat."

"But it should be, shouldn't it? Any relationship…" She bit her lip, color seeping into her cheeks. "Sorry, I know we're not…"

"Having a relationship?" What did she think this *was?* "I'm not scared of the R-word." He just didn't have much experience with it.

"Okay, good to know. But I want to help you, Quinn. Like you've helped me."

He felt himself tensing. "Help me how?"

"I don't know unless you tell me. But everyone has baggage, you know? You know mine and—"

"I don't know all of yours."

Her eyes widened. "What do you want to know?"

"You told me you were engaged once. What happened there?" Anything to keep her from asking him questions. Wanting to know more about his life and all the mistakes he'd made.

Meghan sat back against the sofa, clearly surprised. "He broke it off."

"You said it was a good thing."

"Yes."

He studied her, wondering what she was reluctant to share. He shouldn't push her, not if he wanted to keep his own secret, and yet he realized he wanted to know. Even if the thought of Meghan with another guy had him clenching his fists. "So why did he break it off?"

She sighed. "Because he realized Polly was going to be part of our lives… forever."

"Polly was the reason he broke it off?" Quinn sat upright, indignation coursing through him. "The guy sounds like a douche."

"To be fair, it was a lot to sign up for. We were only eighteen years old."

"You wanted to get married at eighteen?" It didn't sound like the Meghan he knew, the feisty, fiery independent spirit he'd come to respect and admire.

"I think I wanted someone to take care of me, at least for a little while," she answered slowly. "I suppose I didn't really think it through. Neither of us did. Ben thought Polly would go live with my dad, and I had to disabuse him of that notion."

She smiled faintly and Quinn asked, "Were you tempted? To let Polly live with him? Because no matter what, it can be hard work."

"I know." She lifted her chin, its slight wobble betraying her. "But I don't regret it. And I don't regret things finishing with Ben. I wouldn't have been happy with a man who didn't want Polly along with me." She took a deep breath. "But I realize that's a lot to ask of someone, which is why I'm happy with something more… temporary." She let her gaze rest on his, the meaning clear. What they had wasn't meant to last. It might be more than a fling or a one-night stand, but it wasn't the real deal.

Except Quinn kind of felt like it was.

"So," she said lightly. "You know all about my sorry engagement." She paused, her head cocked, her eyes gentle. "You're sure you're okay about the river?"

"Sure." Quinn waved a hand dismissively. "I'm fine."

"You can tell me, Quinn—" she began, but he shook his head. He didn't want to tell Meghan anything. Because while he might be ready to sign up for the real deal, he was pretty sure Meghan wouldn't be, if he let all those secrets slip.

CHAPTER SIXTEEN

S ATURDAY WAS ONE of those perfect spring days, the sky cloudless blue, the air unseasonably warm. Hannah had gone all out and packed a huge, old-fashioned picnic hamper, a wicker basket straight out of one of her glossy magazine shoots, and Polly was practically jumping up and down as they boarded the boat docked behind Sam and Hannah's house.

Quinn wasn't looking so good. Meghan had been sneaking him glances as they'd walked towards the river; his stride had been as easy and loose-limbed as always, but she sensed a tension in him, felt it in herself. He might not remember his father's accident, but she suspected that some part of his subconscious knew exactly what had happened here, and she regretted accepting Hannah's invitation.

"You okay?" she murmured as he handed the picnic basket up to Hannah.

"Sure." He shrugged, his gaze not meeting hers. "Why wouldn't I be?" He didn't wait for an answer as he helped Polly get into the boat, and then Meghan. Finally he got in himself, and Sam told him to sit up front, where he could really feel the waves.

Quinn nodded, his jaw tight, and settled himself on the seat. Meghan joined him, Polly at her side; she loved the way the boat bumped through the crests.

"Have you been on a lot of boats?" she asked as Sam guided them away from the dock and toward the center of the river.

"A fair few." Quinn squinted as he glanced toward the horizon. The surface of the river sparkled with sunlight, and a little breeze was starting to whip the hair about their faces.

"When we clear the islands, we'll really let loose," Sam called, and Hannah waved from her seat next to his.

Meghan glanced again at Quinn, but he didn't look at her. His hand, she saw, was clenched on his thigh, the knuckles white.

Sam navigated past the islands to a straight stretch of river and then he let the throttle go. The boat leapt forward, flying over the waves, spray stinging their faces. Polly crowed with happiness as she rested her hands on the side of the boat, her face lifted to the spray.

Meghan kept one hand on her sister's back as she closed her eyes and reveled in the sunshine. She opened her eyes and looked down at the swells of water, foaming white and green-black underneath. Then she glanced at Quinn and swore aloud.

"*Quinn*—" His face was chalk-white, sweat beading on his forehead as he doubled over. Meghan scrambled across the seat to sit next to him, one arm around his shoulders. "It's okay."

"I'm fine," he said through clenched teeth. "It's just—" Abruptly he jerked away from her and was sick off the side of the boat.

Sam noticed and eased up on the throttle. "Sorry, man. Too fast for you?"

Quinn eased back, wiping his mouth. His eyes were like chips of agate. "Yeah," he said, his voice toneless. "Must be."

"Why don't we have our picnic?" Meghan suggested. Her voice sounded high and anxious. They'd only been out on the water for twenty minutes, but she didn't care. She wanted to get Quinn on dry land.

Hannah was glancing quizzically at them both, concern furrowing her forehead, but Sam nodded easily enough. "Sure thing. There's an island about five minutes from here where we can set up." He glanced at Quinn. "That okay?"

"It's fine," Quinn said. He shot Meghan an irritated glance. "I'm fine."

All right, so maybe she was babying him a little bit. But she was *concerned*. Didn't he realize that?

They didn't speak as Sam guided the boat at a snail's pace towards a deserted island in the middle of the river, nothing more than a few cedars sticking up out of a large chunk of rock.

Sam moored the boat and Hannah scrambled off it, setting up their picnic on a large, flat rock that hung out over the water.

"Are you—" Meghan began, and Quinn's breath hissed from beneath his teeth.

"Would you leave it, Meghan? I'm fine." He jumped out of the boat and then turned around to help Polly. Meghan decided to do as he said and drop it. She couldn't make Quinn open up. If this was how he was defining their relationship, then she'd have to go with that. But it stung more than a little, to see how he was closing her out.

Sam and Hannah deliberately kept the conversation light as they ate, and Meghan did her best to follow their lead. Clearly her anxiety hadn't been helping matters, and after a while Quinn seemed to relax, rather than just act as if he was. Meghan was starting to notice the difference.

After lunch Sam and Quinn went with Polly to explore the other side of the small island, and Hannah and Meghan packed up their picnic things.

"Is Quinn all right?" Hannah asked in a low voice.

"He's determined to be," Meghan answered. She tried to fasten the lid on a Tupperware container and realized her hands were shaking. She forced them to still, knowing her obvious worry would only annoy Quinn now.

"What do you mean?" Hannah asked. "Does he not enjoy the water—"

"Oh Hannah, it's the river," Meghan cut across her, her voice low and yet throbbing. "His father drowned on this river. If the stories are true, *Quinn* almost drowned on this river."

Hannah put one hand up to her mouth. "I'm such an idiot—"

"You weren't to know—"

"But I did know. Everyone knows—"

"Which makes it seem less real, I think," Meghan answered. "At least it did for me. It's always been a story, the backdrop to the town's history, tragic and sad but also kind of distant." She shook her head, her lips pressed together. "But it's not for Quinn. He says he doesn't remember any of it, but I think he does. The feeling, at least. The fear." And her heart ached for him.

"Poor Qu—"

"*Don't* say anything to him," Meghan cut her off fiercely. "Not one word, Hannah. He's private about this. Even to me."

Hannah nodded, her expression serious. "I won't say anything."

A little while later Sam, Quinn, and Polly came back, Polly with her arms full of pretty rocks and pebbles she'd collected. They got back in the boat, and thankfully no one asked Quinn if he'd be all right on the journey back.

Meghan busied herself with Polly, knowing Quinn wanted his space even though it hurt to give it to him. She wanted to help and support him, but it seemed Quinn didn't want her to, and there wasn't much she could do about that. So she kept her arm around Polly and lifted her face to the sunshine and spray, trying to ignore the intensifying ache in her heart.

Back on the shore Quinn made his excuses, saying he needed to do some more work on the hotel. It was the first time he'd brushed her off, and Meghan felt the sting. But she accepted it, because she didn't know what else to do, and she was trying to give Quinn what he wanted without breaking her heart.

She ended up doing errands with Polly, catching up on shopping and laundry until her sister started to complain about being dragged in and out of the house and car. Meghan was just about to turn on yet another episode of *Amazing Wedding Cakes* when she paused.

"Hey, Poll, how would you like to do some baking with Janet?"

Half an hour later she'd dropped Polly off with Janet and was heading toward the hotel, her heart beating hard. Seemed she couldn't accept a brushoff after all.

She knocked on the kitchen door of the hotel but there was no answer, and Meghan didn't even pause before she opened it and stepped into the empty kitchen.

She walked slowly through the house, surprised and a little unnerved by its silence, wondering where Quinn was. His mud-splattered truck was outside. She didn't think he'd have gone far.

As she mounted the stairs, she heard the screech of boards being ripped from the floor. She followed the noise all the way down the hall, and then stood in the doorway watching Quinn destroy the better part of a bedroom.

His t-shirt was soaked through with sweat and he worked methodically, ripping up floorboards and tossing them aside. It seemed like sensible work, yet Meghan saw how hard he was at it, as if he could outrun his mind. His memories. At least that's what she thought was happening, and she knew well enough that you couldn't.

"Quinn." She didn't think he'd heard her but then he stilled, wiping the sweat from his forehead with the back of his arm before he tossed the crowbar aside.

"What are you doing here?"

"I'm worried about you."

"Meghan—"

Her name was a warning. Meghan stepped into the room. "I know you don't want me to be, but I am. That's part of the deal, Quinn."

"I thought you understood our deal."

"Oh, so now you're going to shut me out?" she demanded, her voice vibrating with emotion. "After I cry on your shoulder and you make me dinner and take care of both me and Polly? After all that, the second I start coming back at you, you're going to go cold? Is that how this works?"

He turned to face her, his face stony and blank. "I'm not going cold."

"Feels like freezing to me."

He shook his head impatiently. "Look, I'm not up for

some rehash of my past, okay? I don't remember—"

"You remember," Meghan said quietly. "You remembered about Christmas, and you remembered something out there on the water. I know you did, Quinn, and I wish to hell you'd tell me about it. It's too much for one person to bear alone. I can see that clearly, even if you can't."

He stared at her, his face all hard, grim lines, and Meghan felt as if she were battering a brick wall. There was no getting in.

"Please, Quinn," she said softly. "Why push me away now? You've helped me. Let me help you. Ease the burden, just a little bit."

Still he stared at her, his expression unrelenting. "What can you do?" he finally burst out, the violence of his voice making her blink and recoil just a little. "What can you *do?* You can't change the past. You can't undo it."

"Talking can help—"

"Talking about what? About how my father died? About how it was my fault?"

"Quinn—"

"Don't." He flung out a hand as if to ward her off. "*Don't.* I can't stand pity, Meghan. I can't stand it."

"You think that's what this is? Pity? Because I can't stand it, either. But there's a difference between pity and compassion, Quinn."

"Doesn't feel like it to me."

"Why won't you let me in?" she demanded. "Does it feel

better to bear this alone? To be the tough guy? Is that what this is about? Pride?" Her voice rang out and they stared at each other for a full, tense minute, neither of them blinking.

"This isn't about pride," Quinn finally said quietly. "It's about staying sane."

"Maybe you need to go a little crazy," Meghan answered. "Just for a bit. Otherwise you just stuff it all down and it doesn't go away. It's going to pop up sometime when it's *really* inconvenient." She gave him the ghost of a smile. "Trust me, I know how that goes."

"Do you?"

"I'm not a hundred percent cured, I'm not saying that. You know as well as I do that I'm still dealing with all my baggage. But please, *please* let me help you deal with yours."

She held her breath, waiting, hoping, praying... and then he spoke.

"I remembered," he said flatly. "Okay? I remembered the accident. I remembered falling into the water. An ice fishing hole. It was so dark and cold and the water filled my mouth and I felt like I was choking—" He broke off with a shudder, doubling over, his arms wrapped around himself.

"Oh Quinn. *Quinn.*" Meghan came to him, wrapping her arms around him, her cheek pressed against his back. "It's okay. It's okay now."

"It's not okay," he answered savagely. "It will never be okay. My father's death tore my family apart. It tore this whole damn town apart, and it's *my fault.*"

"You were a child—"

"Doesn't matter. Doesn't change anything." He took a shuddering breath. "You know what else I remember? I remember him reaching for me. I remember grabbing his hand and how the edge of the hole in the ice hit my stomach, ripped through my parka. I remember lying flat on the ice, shaking with cold, and then seeing my father slip and fall in. I saw his face, Meghan, as he fell in. I saw the realization there that I wasn't strong enough to pull him out." His shoulders shook and Meghan held on tight, whispering soothing, nonsense words, trying to tell him in every way that she could that it wasn't his fault.

Eventually he pulled away a little bit, and she let him go. Watched him warily, not sure what would happened now.

"Do you have an hour?" he asked, his voice gravelly with emotion.

She didn't hesitate. "Yes."

"Then let's get out of here. Out of Creighton Falls. I want to go to a place where I feel like I can breathe."

She followed him downstairs and then outside, into his truck. It was late afternoon but the air was still warm, the sun still shining in a bright blue sky.

"Where do you want to go?" Meghan asked as Quinn pulled out of the parking lot.

"Anywhere that's not here." He gave her a wobbly smile. "Is there somewhere to get a decent cup of coffee?"

She considered. "Clayton, maybe."

"Janet mentioned Clayton. Said it was still a tourist attraction."

"Oh it is," Meghan assured him. "Or what passes for one up here."

"Which way?"

She gave him directions and he headed out of Creighton Falls, taking Route 12 along the river to Clayton. They didn't speak, but the silence didn't feel awkward or uncomfortable, just peaceful. After about ten minutes in the truck, Quinn took her hand in his, resting it on his thigh as he drove. Meghan leaned her head back against the seat and just let herself be.

In Clayton they parked across from one of the marinas and Quinn bought them both coffees from a cute little shop along the river. They walked along the promenade, the breeze buffeting their faces. Meghan waited for Quinn to speak first.

"Thank you," he said gruffly. "For calling me on my shit."

"No problem," Meghan answered with a smile. "Anytime."

He laughed, shaking his head as he took a sip of coffee. It felt good to hear him laugh; already he'd lost a little of that tormented look, as if an endless reel of memory was playing in his head.

"It came on so suddenly," he said after a moment. "The memory. One second I was staring out at the water, and the next I felt like I was drowning. Literally... it was as if I was reliving it." He grimaced. "I didn't think that kind of thing actually happened."

"Memory is a powerful thing."

"Yeah."

She hesitated, sensing that Quinn would happily leave it at that. "Why do you think it was your fault, Quinn?"

He didn't answer for a moment, just squinted out at the river. "Looks beautiful now, doesn't it?" he asked with a nod towards the water that sparkled with sunlight. "Pretty damn peaceful."

"Quinn—"

"I've always known it was my fault. I may not have remembered the accident, but I sure as hell remembered *that.*"

"What do you mean—"

"I was the one who begged my dad to go ice fishing. I was the one who was fooling around on the ice, too near the hole. I was the one who fell."

"But you were six, and it was an accident—"

"I get what you're trying to tell me, Meghan," he said. "I do. I know I was just a kid. I know I can't really blame myself, not like that. But..." He blew out a breath. "The reality is, if I hadn't fallen, my dad wouldn't have died. Nothing can change that."

"No," Meghan agreed quietly. "But you don't have to live your life hostage to that fact."

His mouth quirked up at the corner although his eyes

still looked lightless and bleak. "What makes you think I'm doing that?"

"I don't know…" She really didn't. It was just a guess, a gut feeling maybe, that his carefree attitude and nomadic lifestyle were related to his father's accident. That he'd spent his life running away.

"I just remembered this morning," Quinn said lightly. "I'd hardly call my life *hostage.*"

"Right." She shot him a guiltily apologetic smile. "I'm overreacting and clearly *not* helping. Sorry."

"Don't be." He reached out one hand and pulled her toward him for a quick kiss. Afterward he rested his forehead against hers, and they stood there, breathing each other in. Meghan felt like she could have stayed like that forever.

Then Quinn eased back with a tired smile. "Come on," he said, slinging his arm around her shoulders. "Let's go home."

CHAPTER SEVENTEEN

"I HAVE TO go away."

Quinn watched Meghan's face go white and mentally cursed his clumsy intro. Truth, he was a little nervous. "I don't mean—just for the weekend, that's all."

"Oh." Her expression cleared but she still looked a little wary. "Where? Back to New York?"

"Yes." Quinn jammed his hands in the pocket of his jeans and gazed around the hotel's empty living room with its fresh floorboards and stripped walls. It looked clean and empty, a place, perhaps, of promise. "It's my mother's seventieth birthday, and we're having a family dinner."

"Oh. Right."

"And actually…" He took a deep breath, amazed at how nervous he was. What was he, twelve? "I was wondering if you wanted to come with me?"

Meghan's eyes widened. "To—"

"New York. Yes. For the weekend." She was still staring at him, and so he continued, practically tripping over the words, "Think five star hotel, strawberries dipped in chocolate, and a bathtub of champagne."

She let out an uncertain laugh. "Wow. Okay."

"I know there's Polly to think of," he continued quickly. "But I thought maybe, if you prepared her enough, she could stay with Janet for the weekend. Because you can't be there twenty-four seven forever, no matter what happens this weekend."

"I know."

Her quick agreement took him by surprise. "So…"

"New York City." She let out another uncertain laugh. "I've never actually been there."

"So now's your chance. Penthouse of the Waldorf Astoria all the way."

"Seriously?"

"Seriously."

"You are one tempting offer, Quinn Freeman."

He gave her one of his old, cocky grins. "That I am."

She let out a shaky breath and ran her hand through her hair, leaving it adorably tousled. "I want to say yes. Just… let me think about it first."

"Okay," Quinn answered lightly, as if it didn't matter so much, as if he wasn't practically sweating through his shirt. "It's only Monday."

"Right." Meghan stared at him for a moment, smiling uncertainly, and Quinn felt as if he'd just taken their relationship to a whole new level. It wasn't a bad thing, but… whoa.

"Okay," Meghan said at last. "I should finish the patch

upstairs."

"Okay." Quinn nodded vaguely towards the entire hotel. "I should… work."

"Right." She gave him a quick, playful smile and then headed upstairs. Quinn glanced around the empty room and expelled a shaky breath.

"HE ASKED YOU to go to New York with him? To meet his family?" Hannah stared at Meghan, her jaw well and truly dropped. "You said yes, I hope?"

"I said… probably." Meghan leaned her head against the sofa in the Taylors' kitchen and cradled the cup of tea Hannah had just handed her. She'd come over here in her lunch break, needing her friend's advice and perspective.

"Probably? Why probably?"

"Because I need to make sure I have Polly taken care of. And… because it feels like a big deal." Meghan blew out a breath. "I mean, dinner with the *Freemans.*"

"I know. Wow. You'll need a new dress."

"I feel like I need new everything. Do you know what the state of my underwear drawer is?"

Hannah's eyes danced as she took a sip of tea. "Surely Quinn's seen your underwear."

"Yes, but it feels different now. I mean, a fling in Creighton Falls versus a weekend with his family in the city, and staying in the penthouse suite of the Waldorf Astoria?" Meghan shook her head. "I feel so… gauche. So unprepared."

"But Quinn likes you as you are," Hannah reminded her. "Maybe even loves you—"

"We haven't said that to each other."

Hannah raised her eyebrows. "Yet?"

"I… I don't know." She hadn't let herself think about loving Quinn, whether she loved him or he loved her. But now, with this invitation, she felt as if he'd given their relationship—and they'd barely begun using that word—a whole new status. It was exciting and terrifying all at once, and she was filled with both hope and fear as to whether this could actually work. Quinn Freeman inhabited a whole different world than she did. Creighton Falls was a detour for him, an aberration. It was her reality.

"Don't overthink it," Hannah advised. "Really, Meghan. Just… go with it. And see what happens."

"Easy advice from the happily married woman," Meghan answered with a sigh. "You've reached the other side. This is scary stuff, Hannah."

Hannah's face softened. "Are you afraid of getting hurt?"

"Isn't everybody?" Meghan retorted. "Sometimes relationships feel like death wishes. Do they ever end well?"

"You've had one bad experience—"

"I've had a lot of experience of people walking away," Meghan returned flatly, staring into the depths of her tea to hide the bleakness she could feel on her face. "Just about everyone who mattered to me at one point. I know that doesn't mean everyone will, and I realize I need to take a risk to make a relationship work and be happy. I am that emotionally aware, thank you very much."

"Then what's keeping you from giving Quinn an unequivocal yes?"

Meghan sighed. "Fear is a powerful thing."

Hannah nodded soberly. "Yes," she agreed. "It is."

And so Meghan adopted an entirely unreasonable process for decision making. She set herself tests—if Janet could take Polly, if Polly was excited about the idea, if there was a sale on lingerie…

The odds were definitely in her favor. Janet was thrilled, Polly was excited, and Victoria's Secret had a fifty percent off clearance sale. She was either doomed or blessed.

On Wednesday she told Quinn she could go. She'd come to the hotel in the late afternoon to finish up some repair work, and Quinn was sanding floorboards in the living room. Meghan stood in the doorway, uneasy and nervous and yet also bubbling with excitement.

"So… that New York thing."

Quinn stilled. "Yeah?"

"I can go. That is, if you still—"

"Of course I still." He strode toward her, pulling her into his arm for a quick yet thorough kiss. "I absolutely still. When can you leave?"

"Anytime on Friday. Janet will meet Polly after work."

"Perfect. Let's leave in the morning, and then we'll have

the rest of the day together. The dinner's not till Saturday."

"Okay."

He kissed her again, fast and fierce and wonderful, and then let her go.

Friday couldn't come soon enough, and yet it also came too soon. Meghan couldn't quite believe how nervous she was. This was Quinn, after all. They'd had some fantastic sex and some fairly intense conversations and she *knew* him. Maybe she was even falling in love with him. But she was still nervous.

Over the last few days she'd started to daydream, just a little. She pictured Quinn staying in Creighton Falls, reopening the hotel or even just bartending somewhere. Something to make him stay put. She pictured them together in her little ranch house, or even in a bigger house they'd buy together. She even pictured the wedding ring, the dress.

Then she put a stop to those fantasies because she knew they were dangerous. And like Hannah said, she didn't want to overthink this. Even if she already had.

Friday morning was bright and warm, the sunshine sparkling on the river, the buds starting to come out on the trees. Sam was seriously annoyed because the maple syrup season had been so short, but Meghan was grateful for the unseasonably warm weather. She'd bought a cocktail dress from the department store in Watertown and it was skimpy and sleeveless.

Quinn picked her up in his old mud-splattered truck,

throwing her bag in the back. "Hop in," he said, and Meghan did.

"Are you going to drive this all the way into Manhattan?"

"Nope, just to Watertown where my Beamer's parked."

She laughed. "Seriously?"

"I have a certain standard to maintain," Quinn informed her with a grin. "Showing up to my mother's townhouse on Fifth Avenue in this truck would not cut it."

"Of course not." And what about her truck? What about *her?* She pushed her fears down, determined to enjoy the day.

And it was, in the end, remarkably easy to enjoy the day. Cruising down 81 in Quinn's Beamer, the windows down, her hair blowing in the wind, his arm around her shoulders… well, it didn't really get better than that, did it?

Except it did. They arrived in New York and after tossing the keys to the hotel's valet, Quinn whisked her up to the penthouse suite of the Waldorf Astoria, which was bigger than her entire house. By a lot.

Meghan walked slowly through the elegant rooms, marveling at the antiques and amenities, before Quinn tugged her back to the bedroom.

"But I want to see New York…"

"We've got time," he assured her, pulling her onto the bed, and she had to agree that they did.

A very satisfactory hour later, they hit the streets of New York, with Quinn as excited as a little boy, tugging her this way and that, taking her to the Top of the Rock, and then up to Central Park, and then to Pinkberry for frozen yogurt, and then in a taxi to downtown where they looked at Ground Zero and Wall Street, until the sky darkened and Meghan's feet ached and he told her they had to go back to get ready for dinner.

"Dinner? Where?"

"21."

Meghan gulped. "This feels like a fairy tale," she told Quinn. And fairy tales weren't real.

"Then enjoy it," he said. "You deserve a fairy tale, Meghan."

Back at the hotel she soaked in the sunken marble tub until her fingers and toes were as shriveled as prunes, and then slipped on the cranberry-red silk sheath she'd bought and now didn't look nearly as classy as it had when she'd tried it on in Watertown. She tried to pull her hair up in a sophisticated chignon but it didn't really work and so she left it down, reminding herself that Quinn liked her as she was. Thankfully.

"Meghan?" Quinn's voice floated from the suite's living room. "Not to rush, but our reservation is in fifteen minutes."

"I'm ready." Meghan slipped her feet into the black stiletto heels that had been part of her Upstate shopping spree—along with some sexy underwear—and drawing a deep breath, opened the bedroom door.

Quinn was waiting in the living room, gazing out the

windows at the darkening city skyline, and the sight of him left Meghan's mind spinning and speechless. She'd seen him only in his Creighton Falls clothes: flannel shirts, hiking boots, jeans. Tonight he was wearing a crisp white shirt, open at the throat, under a black blazer. Narrow gray suit trousers completed the look, and with his bed-rumpled hair and wicked smile he was the most gorgeous thing she'd ever seen.

"You look amazing," he said, his gaze warm on her, his smile still wicked.

"So do you. You look... like you're supposed to look."

Quinn cocked an eyebrow. "I'm not sure what that means."

"Only that this is your world. You've been in my world for the last few weeks, and now I'm in yours."

"This is only part of my world," he said as he reached for her hands, drawing her toward him. "How do you like it so far?" he murmured against her lips.

It scares me. "I like it just fine," Meghan said, and Quinn kissed her.

They took a cab to the restaurant, and a white-jacketed maître-de ushered them to a private table in the upstairs mural-lined dining room.

"I hope you're hungry," Quinn told her. "There are four courses, and it's an insult to the chef to skip one."

"Of course it is," Meghan murmured. The menu left her dazed: assorted caviars, foie gras terrine, octopus carpaccio.

She was barely aware that such things existed. "Would you hate me if I asked if they had a cheeseburger?" she half-teased and Quinn grinned.

"I dare you."

"Actually, I don't think I could. But I'm not too keen on octopus."

"Have you ever tried it?"

"No, have you?"

"Yeah, once or twice." He smiled, lounging back in his chair. "You're not missing much."

"Do you miss travelling?" Meghan asked impulsively. "Going places, eating strange food, all the adventures... I've never even known what that was like."

"It's been good," Quinn said slowly as he studied the menu. "But... it's not something you can do forever." He lifted his gaze to meet hers and for a moment neither of them said anything. Meghan let the silence stretch on, not daring to ask him what he could do forever—or who with. Quinn might think she deserved the fairy tale, but this was only for the weekend.

They kept the conversation light after that, chatting easily, enjoying the food, all four courses of it, at least mostly. Meghan decided she wasn't fond of foie gras but the filet mignon she could eat every night.

It was late by the time they finished the New York cheesecake and chocolate soufflé, followed by petit fours and coffee, and finally cognac. As they headed out into the night, cabs streaming by on Fifth Avenue, Meghan felt relaxed, a little woozy, and very happy.

Quinn took her hand as they walked down the street, enjoying the evening, the air surprisingly fresh for the city, the moon high above them. Meghan felt as if she could burst into song or start dancing down the street.

"I can't remember the last time I felt so free," she said as she turned to Quinn.

"You needed a break."

"Yes, I really think I did." But she didn't want this to be a break. *Take away the trappings—the city, the glamor, the food and the hotel, fine. But don't take away Quinn.*

She took a deep breath, reminding herself not to overthink any of this, and kept walking.

They spent the next morning in bed, preferring to explore each other rather than the sights of Manhattan.

Quinn ordered room service for a late breakfast and they ate in bed, leisurely, laughing, reveling in each other in a way that felt entirely new to Meghan. This wasn't grabbing a moment of pleasure; this was reveling in a lifetime of it. Or so she was starting to hope.

"So this family dinner," Meghan asked when they'd finally rolled out of bed, showered together, and then dressed. "Is it fancy?"

"Do you really think my mother does anything else?" Quinn answered on a laugh. "But don't worry. It shouldn't take too long, and we still have all tomorrow."

"I'm not worried," Meghan answered, even though she was. "But I should be back in Creighton Falls by the late afternoon. I want some time with Polly before bed."

"Of course."

His easy acceptance of the constraints on her life made her feel a rush of emotion, something she was starting to think might just be love. Funny, how such a big thing could sneak up on you. Make you realize how much you'd missed it before. Maybe she'd drum up the nerve to tell him how she felt. Maybe, if she passed the family test tonight, she would.

They spent the afternoon wandering through the Union Square farmers' market and then walking back uptown through Gramercy Park before finally heading back to the penthouse.

Quinn checked his watch with a regretful face. "I should get ready for this dinner."

"Sounds like a plan."

Quinn disappeared into the shower and Meghan took her things to the second bedroom's ensuite bathroom. She wanted to surprise Quinn with how she looked—the black cocktail dress was deceptively simple and understated, and also the most expensive thing she owned. And tonight she'd get the chignon thing right.

She soaked in the tub, humming to herself, trying to quell the nerves squirming in her stomach, before she dressed and then did her makeup and hair. It took three tries to get the chignon to stay put, but she liked the results. She looked elegant, her cheekbones and eyes more pronounced.

She was just putting the finishing touches on her makeup when Quinn knocked on the door.

"Meghan?"

"I'll be right out—"

"Good, I want to give you a kiss before I go."

Meghan stilled, not sure she'd heard him correctly. "Before you go," she repeated, not quite making it a question.

"I'll cab it up to my mother's apartment. I shouldn't be back too late—maybe ten? Wait up for me," he finished with a husky laugh. "Now are you coming out or not?"

Slowly Meghan lowered the lipstick she'd been holding. In the mirror her face looked pale and strained, her eyes huge and dark.

"Meghan?" Quinn asked again, and now he sounded concerned.

"Sorry, I'm in the tub," Meghan called. "I... I didn't realize how late it was. You're going to have to miss out on that kiss."

"Pay me back later?"

"Sure."

She heard him walk away, and then the sound of the door to the suite clicking shut. She closed her eyes, a wash of humiliation and pain washing over her with a force that nearly sent her to her knees.

She'd read it so wrong. How much wrong she didn't

even know. All of it? The relationship? The intensity? *The love?*

Quinn had never been intending to introduce her to his family. He wasn't making her part of his life. He'd just brought her to New York as his bit on the side while he attended some boring family event.

This, Meghan thought dully, opening her eyes to stare at her haggard reflection, was where the fairy tale ended.

CHAPTER EIGHTEEN

Q UINN WASN'T LOOKING forward to his mother's birthday dinner. Once a year he and his brothers called a temporary truce to celebrate their mother's birthday, but it never lasted long. Jake lounged around, acting bored and indifferent, and Adam criticized. Quinn pretended that everything was one big joke. Eventually all their stances wore thin and they took turns sniping at each other until their mother begged them to get along. Fun times.

Tonight Quinn wanted things to be different. He felt different, thanks to Meghan. He'd had the best time of his life this weekend, better than any adventure he'd chased across the globe because he hadn't found a place at home. He wanted more from life now. He wanted to stay put, he wanted to *try.*

And that made him nervous. He'd laid his cards on the table once before, bared his soul and had it stamped on. It hadn't been love, but it had hurt. Having Meghan walk away from him would hurt a lot more. And in any case, he no longer trusted himself, since no one else had. Maybe he wasn't strong enough for the real deal. Did wanting something badly enough make you strong enough to have it? To keep it? Hell if he knew.

"Quinn." Adam greeted him, unsmiling, at the door. "No tie as usual." Adam, as usual, was wearing a three piece suit.

"I hate to disappoint," Quinn said lightly.

"Right," Adam muttered, and turned away.

And so it already had begun. Seemed like there wouldn't be a truce this year. Quinn headed into the formal drawing room, its long sashed windows overlooking Central Park. His mother and Jake were already there; Margo was sipping a thimbleful of sherry and Jake had started on the whiskey.

"I'll have one of those," Quinn said.

"Quinn." Margo gave him a warm smile. "I'm so glad to see you."

That made one person. Jake handed Quinn a tumbler of whiskey. "How are things?" he asked.

"Fine. How's saving the world?"

"Only a little bit of Bolivia," Jake replied with a smile that didn't reach his eyes. Sometimes Quinn wondered what drove Jake to launch rescue mission after rescue mission around the world. He didn't think his brother had had a day off in about ten years. Maybe he was trying to prove something, but Quinn knew how that went. You never did.

"Happy Birthday, Mom," he said, and kissed his mother's cheek. Adam came into the room, surveying everything, frowning slightly as if nothing was quite good enough.

Quinn waited for him to ask about Creighton Falls but Adam didn't say anything.

After drinks they moved into the dining room, where Margo's housekeeper and cook, Dorothy, was bringing in the first course, slices of melon wrapped in prosciutto.

"It's so nice to be all together," Margo said and Quinn wondered if she really believed that, or simply wished it were true. He and his brothers had never gotten along, at least not in his memory. Maybe they had as little kids; he'd never asked about those years and no one had offered any information.

As for the decades since then... he couldn't remember a time when Adam hadn't been sniping at him and Jake hadn't been checking out. Not one.

"So, how's running the world?" he asked Adam who didn't look up from cutting his melon slice into equal segments.

"The same."

It took Quinn half an hour of awkward chat and two courses to realize no one was going to ask him about the hotel or Creighton Falls. It caused a slow burn of anger to lick through him. Did none of them care about the town they'd once called home?

"So," he said when Dorothy had cleared the plates and they were waiting for dessert. "The hotel's coming along pretty well."

It was as if he'd hurled a grenade into the center of the

dining room table. The ensuing silence was taut with the wait for the explosion. Margo bit her lip and Jake lounged back in his chair. Adam dabbed his lips with his napkin, saying nothing.

"If anyone's interested," Quinn continued, an edge entering his voice. "Some of the people up there are really pleased that something's happening with the hotel. They've been helping out—"

"We'll talk about this later," Adam said, iron in his voice. Quinn blinked.

"I thought everyone would like to know—"

"Later, Quinn."

Quinn looked at his mother, who was staring down at her plate. "I met Janet Pierce," he told her, and saw her stiffen. "She asked me to send you her regards."

"*Quinn*—" Adam's voice was a snarl.

"It's all right, Adam." Her face pale, her smile fragile, Margo looked at her sons. "Tell Janet hello," she said, her voice no more than a whisper. "Please."

Half an hour later Adam called Quinn into the study as if he were a recalcitrant schoolboy.

"What the hell was that about?" he demanded.

"What? Are we going to pretend the hotel doesn't exist?"

"We've been doing that for the last twenty years," Adam snapped. "I see no reason to stop."

"Don't you think it's all a bit… dysfunctional?" Quinn suggested quietly. Adam's lips compressed, the skin around them white.

"It's worked."

"Do you really think—"

"You've kept the repairs under ten grand, I assume?"

"Of your money, yes," Quinn retorted. He'd spent a fair bit of his own on the hotel, but he didn't begrudge a cent of it.

Adam shook his head slowly. "I never wanted to think about that place ever again."

"Don't you have any good memories of it?" Quinn asked quietly. Adam didn't answer.

"I've procured a local real estate agent," he said after clearing his throat. "He thinks there might be an interested buyer."

Quinn blinked, shocked by the suddenness of Adam's announcement. "Wait... what? Who's the buyer?"

"This is the ironic part," he said flatly. "They want to raze the building and use the land for a truck dealership."

Quinn stared at his brother in disbelief. "A truck dealership?" He pictured a huge monstrosity of a modern building, the grass concreted over for a hundred monster trucks, and felt sick with rage. "There are zoning laws—"

Adam's mouth flattened once again. "The real estate agent assures me they can be dealt with, and the local councilors will be sympathetic, especially since the town is so economically deprived."

"A truck dealership on the green will ruin the town—"

"As far as I can tell the town was already heading toward ruin. What did you think was going to happen, Quinn? You've done the work. It's over now."

"It's *not* over—"

"Go back to Thailand," Adam said wearily. "Or wherever you feel like jetting off to next. Isn't that what you always do?"

Quinn stared at his brother, something very close to hatred churning like acid in his stomach. He'd known Adam was controlling, had known this would happen all along, and yet...

It still hurt. It still infuriated him, because he didn't want to let go of the hotel, or the town, or the woman he loved. He'd let Adam bully him into giving up everything once before. He didn't want to do it this time.

Yet what could he do? Adam held all the cards. He always had.

"Well?" Adam asked. "What are you waiting for?"

Quinn's throat worked and insults and accusations bubbled up inside him. "Nothing," he managed, his voice strangled, and then he turned and walked out, slamming the door behind him.

MEGHAN HAD ALL evening to go over the last few days and realize what a fool she'd been. Quinn had never actually invited her to the family dinner. She'd just assumed. And he'd assumed she wouldn't go, that it didn't even need clarifying, which made her feel worse.

She had an awful feeling she'd misread everything that had happened in the last few weeks. She'd gone in with her eyes wide open, had known it was only a fling, and yet... the heart was ever deceitful. Because somewhere along the way she'd started buying into the fairy tale. She'd told herself she wasn't, that she was just dreaming a little, but Meghan knew now she'd bought into the thing completely. Let herself believe in happily-ever-after.

By eleven o'clock she knew Quinn would be back soon and she had no idea how to face him. What to say, to admit. She considered trying to act as normal, pretend she was fine, but she didn't think she had the strength. And she was too hurt not to want to let him know, even if it would be humiliating. Even if Quinn had no idea he'd hurt her.

She'd been so *stupid.*

She heard the sound of the door opening and then footsteps. Quinn came into the living room of the suite, his shoulders slumped, his expression grim.

Meghan, curled up in a chair in the corner of the room, tensed. "Quinn...?"

"Hey." He raked a hand through his hair and gave her a tired smile. "Sorry, it went on longer than I thought."

"How was it?"

"Just the usual." He turned away from her to shed his coat and Meghan realized he wasn't going to say anything else. More proof she'd never really been part of his life. He didn't want her to be. And yet even so she saw how careworn he looked and she wanted to comfort him.

"The usual?" she asked, trying to keep her voice light and unable to. "Judging by your face, that's not a good thing."

"Yeah. Well." Quinn jammed his hands in the pockets of his trousers, hunching his shoulders. "I'm just tired." He found a smile somewhere and put it on his face. "How was your evening?"

Horrible. She found a smile too, just as forced and fake as his. "Okay. Lonely."

"Sorry."

"Yeah. Well." An echo of his dismissal. Everything stung.

Quinn reached an arm out toward her. "Come to bed."

Meghan lifted her hand to his, and it felt as if she were hefting a leaden weight. He pulled her to her feet and she came slowly, her mind resisting even if her body didn't. Could she really do this? Pretend he hadn't hurt her, that nothing had changed? Was that the kind of relationship they had?

Quinn slipped his arms around her waist, resting his chin on top of her head. "I'm glad to be back with you," he whispered.

"Are you?" Two short, sharp words that came from her mouth like bullets, spewing cynicism. Meghan felt Quinn stiffen. So she couldn't pretend everything was okay. The realization brought both fear and relief.

"Meghan…?" Quinn's voice was wary.

Meghan drew a deep breath and pulled away from him. She felt alarmingly close to tears. "Look, Quinn, I knew what this was when we started it. But I guess…" Another deep breath, this one revealingly ragged. "I guess I started thinking we were going somewhere with this."

Quinn stared at her, his eyes veiled, his face guarded. "Where is this coming from?"

"Where do you think it's coming from? I don't know where we are. *No.*" She held up a hand, the hurt now replaced by anger. "Actually, I do know. I realized when you walked out of the hotel for your big family dinner."

Quinn shook his head slowly. "What are you trying to say, Meghan?"

"Why didn't you invite me?" she burst out, cringing inwardly at how hurt she sounded. "I thought—I thought when you invited me to New York for the weekend, you'd introduce me to your family. I thought you were taking our relationship to another level—"

"I *was*—"

"But you just wanted me here as an extended booty call."

"That is *not* true." Quinn's eyes flashed with an anger of his own. "I don't know why you would think it was."

"Because you separate me from the rest of your life! You can come into my house, get my sister to care about you, but I can't even meet your family."

Quinn's jaw bunched. "It's not like that."

"It feels very much like that to me, Quinn." Weary now,

Meghan shook her head. "I don't know why I'm even arguing this. I realized tonight that we never had anything real between us."

"You realized that just because I didn't invite you to a dinner?" Quinn demanded. "Seriously, Meghan?"

"It was telling—"

"It was *one thing*. Is that how a relationship works? The minute something goes wrong you decide it wasn't real?"

Meghan stared at him, bewildered now. "What are you saying?"

"I'm saying I thought we had more going on here than you seem to believe. I care about you—"

"What does that even mean, Quinn? Where can we go from here? You're still going to sell the hotel. You're not sticking around in Creighton Falls, and I'm not leaving."

He stared at her for a long moment. "Is that an ultimatum?"

She sighed, deflated. "No, just a fact. I don't really see how we can have a future. Our lives are too different."

"They don't have to be different."

She arched an eyebrow, clinging to her skepticism even as hope leapt inside of her. "What do you suggest?"

"What's keeping you in Creighton Falls?"

"So I'm the one who has to change?"

"I'm just asking, Meghan—"

"My job. My family. My life. You're the one who bums around the world. Why don't *you* change?"

Quinn's face paled and hurt flashed in his eyes. "At least now I know what you think of me."

"I didn't mean it like that—"

"I think you did." He turned away from her, and Meghan stared at him in frustration. She knew she wasn't being fair. Nothing he said would satisfy her now. "Quinn, look, maybe I'm being unreasonable, but the truth is I'm hurt. It hurt that you didn't invite me to that stupid dinner." Her voice trembled and she blinked rapidly. "The truth is I was dressed and ready to go when you said goodbye. I'd assumed you'd invited me, and you'd assumed I wouldn't go. Maybe you're ashamed of me, the hick from the sticks—"

"Oh, Meghan." In two long strides Quinn was across the room, taking her into his arms. "I'm sorry. I'm such an ass."

"But it's true, isn't it?" Meghan asked shakily. "You've kept me separate from your life. You didn't even want to tell me about your memories."

Quinn let out a shuddering sigh, his arms still around her, his chin resting on top of her head. "The truth is," he said after a moment, and then stopped. Meghan waited, sensing the struggle inside him. "The truth is," he started again, his voice low and husky, "I didn't invite you to the dinner tonight because I didn't want you to meet my family. Not because I'm ashamed of you, but because *they're* ashamed of *me.*"

It took Meghan a few seconds to absorb the meaning of his words. "Ashamed of you?" She tried to pull away from him a little but Quinn held her fast. "What do you mean? Why?"

"Because I'm a screw-up," he stated flatly. "I always have been. I fooled around in school, I got in trouble countless times, nearly expelled from boarding school, and then a college dropout. The one time I tried..." His voice choked and he stopped abruptly.

Meghan eased back to look in his face. "The one time you tried?" she repeated softly.

"When I was a junior in college, I came to Adam with a business proposal. I wanted to work for Freeman Enterprises. I had ideas, and my father had left us all with thirty percent of the company, and my mother the last ten. Adam shot me down."

His jaw hardened, his gaze distant and veiled. "Shot you down? How?"

Quinn shrugged restlessly. "He dismissed my ideas and refused to let me work for the company. Said I was too much of a screw-up, which I was, but I wanted to change. I wanted to give something back. I laid it all out there for him, told him what I regretted and what I wanted, and still I got a big flat no." He drew a quick, ragged breath. "So I went to my mother and Jake to get their votes and force Adam's hand."

He stopped, seeming as if he wouldn't say any more, and Meghan prompted quietly, "And what happened then?"

"They voted against me. Seventy percent to my thirty to keep me out of the company. I suppose I deserved it. I hadn't done all that much to recommend myself, but I guess I wanted a chance."

"And so instead you dropped out of college and took off to see the world."

"Seemed like a good idea at the time."

"Oh, Quinn." Meghan placed a hand on his cheek and he closed his eyes. "I'm sorry."

"Not your fault."

"Even so."

"I can't really blame them," he said in a low voice. "I've never done a decent thing in my life."

"I think you've done a lot of decent things," Meghan said quietly. "I've seen the decent things you've done, Quinn. I've benefitted from them, and so has everyone in Creighton Falls."

He let out a laugh that sounded more like despair. "They won't when the hotel is sold, Meghan. Adam informed me tonight. He's engaged a real estate agent and there's already a potential buyer."

She tensed in his arms. "Who—"

"Someone who wants to raze the hotel and turn the property into a truck dealership."

Shock blazed through her, followed by fury. "What? No." She wriggled out of his arms. "Quinn, you can't let that happen."

"I can't stop it."

"You've got to explain to your brother—"

"I just told you how that worked before," Quinn said, anger edging his voice.

Meghan stared at the man she knew she loved, saw the despair and failure in his face, and thought, *no.* She was not going to let this happen to her town. She wasn't going to let this happen to *Quinn.* "Maybe it's time for it to work now," she said.

"Meghan—"

"Why let your brother have his way, Quinn? Why take this lying down?"

"I don't have a choice—"

"You always have a choice whether to fight or not." She took a deep breath, summoning all of her courage. "But I think you've chosen not to fight for a long time."

Quinn stilled for a second. "That's because I fought and lost."

"So get up again. One round isn't the whole fight. You can come out swinging again."

"And have my family vote against me again?"

"Maybe they won't this time. You're not a twenty-year-old college student, Quinn. You're a grown man who has proved his staying power. Why not fight this time, for something you really believe in?"

"It's not that simple."

"Just because something is simple doesn't mean it isn't hard. But you know what I think?"

Quinn folded his arms, his expression stony. "I think

you're going to tell me."

"Damn straight I am. I think you've taken the no-responsibility route because it's easier than trying and failing. I think you've acted like you don't care because it's safer than showing you do and getting hurt. But what kind of life is that, Quinn? How many bars are you going to mix drinks for, how many women are you going to seduce and then walk away from? It's not real life. It hasn't made you happy."

A muscle ticked in his jaw. "And you know all this how—?"

"I'm guessing," Meghan admitted. "Because I've come to know you. And the man I know, the man I care about, wouldn't walk away from this."

"And what is 'this'? A hotel that's half falling down?"

"A place and a project you believe in. Why shouldn't it be a proper hotel again?" Meghan cried. "Why shouldn't you make it one? You've got the whole town behind you, Quinn, if you'd just believe in yourself. Believe how good and strong and wise you are. Please." She placed a hand on his arm. "Please believe me. I think you're amazing. I know it. And you can do this, if you want to."

Quinn stared down at her hand on his arm; her fingers were trembling. "You give a pretty good pep talk," he finally said grudgingly, and she let out a wild laugh. "Maybe lifestyle coach can be your backup career plan."

"Maybe," she agreed, her heart sailing high on wings of hope.

"Still don't see how I'm supposed to convince my brother of all this."

"You'll find a way," Meghan insisted. "It can't end like this. It just can't."

Quinn sighed and placed his hand over hers. "Sometimes it does, Meghan. You and I both know happy endings aren't for everybody." He looked at her sadly, and she felt her stomach lurch, her fledgling hope-filled heart start to plummet.

"Are they for us?" she whispered. Quinn didn't answer for a long moment. Meghan closed her eyes, bracing herself against the wave of pain she could feel about to crash over her.

"I don't know," he finally admitted, and her heart seesawed crazily, not knowing whether that was good or bad news. "This is new to me, Meghan. You and me, dealing with my family, standing up for something I believe in... all of it is new. And I'm not sure..." He trailed off, his arms tightening around her, giving her the courage to prompt,

"You're not sure about what, Quinn?"

"I'm not sure if I'm strong enough. For any of it."

She tightened her arms around him, wielding him to her. "You are," she said. "I know you are, even if you don't. And really by now, you should trust that I'm right."

He laughed softly. "You think so, huh?"

"I know so."

Quinn breathed in deeply, his lips brushing her hair. "Okay," he said, and to Meghan it sounded like a promise.

CHAPTER NINETEEN

THEY LEFT FOR Creighton Falls the next morning. They didn't talk any more about the future, no heavy subjects at all, but Meghan felt the atmosphere tauten with expectation. With both hope and fear.

They held hands as Quinn drove up Highway 81, the sun shining benevolently down on them, surely a good sign. A thousand questions burned on Meghan's tongue—she ached to know what Quinn planned to do—but she kept them to herself. Quinn knew what she wanted and hoped for. Now it was his turn to act.

At Watertown Quinn parked the Beamer back in the garage and picked up the truck. Climbing into the well-worn interior felt like shedding one skin and taking on another. The real one.

They didn't talk as Quinn drove into Creighton Falls, the sun gone, the sky now heavy with clouds, raindrops spattering against the windshield. He pulled into her driveway and Meghan turned to him, a question in her eyes.

"Do you want to…?"

"I've got a lot to do back at the hotel," Quinn answered

with a shake of his head. "A lot to think about."

"Okay." She managed a shaky smile. "I should pick Polly up and catch up on laundry and stuff, anyway." He leaned over to give her a quick kiss but Meghan felt his heart wasn't in it. Not that she was paranoid or anything. Not that she was terrified that if she gave Quinn an inch of space he'd take three hundred miles, all the way back to the city.

She heard his truck drive away as she closed the front door behind her, the house quiet and dark. Polly was still at Janet's, and Meghan had had a few updates throughout the weekend to say she was okay. She'd take a few minutes to throw in a load of laundry and look through the mail before going to pick her up.

She was not going to obsess over Quinn, and what he needed to think about. Whether he needed to think about her, and whether he wanted her in his life.

She drove to Janet's and was greeted by Polly at the door; her sister squealed and jumped up and down as Meghan came into the hall.

"Meghan, Meghan, I had a hot dog and a chocolate milkshake and they were so good."

"A hot dog?" Meghan raised her eyebrows at Janet as she hugged her sister. "Wow, something different."

"Yes, your father took her to a baseball game down in Watertown yesterday," Janet said. "They had such a nice time."

"He did?" Meghan stared at Janet blankly.

"I hope it was okay? I ran into him at the Price Chopper on Friday night and he mentioned it so I said he should go ahead and buy the tickets. And he did."

"Wow." Meghan shook her head slowly. In the ten years that Meghan had been Polly's primary caregiver, her father had never stepped up like that. Never taken her sister anywhere. But maybe that was because she hadn't let him. She'd never encouraged him, because she hadn't trusted him, hadn't wanted to be let down again.

But maybe she'd been the one letting her father down.

"That's great," she said at last, her mind still reeling. "I'm glad they had a good time together."

"Can we go again?" Polly asked. "Except I didn't like all the noise, when everybody cheered."

"Knowing the Watertown Bucks, that won't happen too often," Meghan joked, and Polly stared at her, nonplussed.

"What does that mean?"

"Sorry, Poll, I was just being silly. Maybe next time you can bring earmuffs." There had been a period of a couple years in Polly's childhood when earmuffs had been a regular accessory. "Thank you, Janet," Meghan said, turning to give the older woman a hug.

"You had a nice time?"

"An amazing time." And an emotional and overwhelming time, but she wouldn't go into details now. "Come on, Poll. Let's get you home."

QUINN WALKED THROUGH the empty rooms of the hotel, his footsteps echoing in the stillness. Instead of mold and rot, the rooms smelled of fresh wood and plaster. The hotel would still need a lot of work if it was ever to operate again, but he'd made a good start.

He stood in the living room with the ornate fireplace and high ceiling and imagined a wrecking ball swinging through the window. Pictured the place leveled and concrete poured in its place, the village green overrun with shiny new trucks. He hated the thought. Hated it with a savage fury that surprised him; for so long he'd kept himself from feeling anything but faint bemusement.

Meghan was right; he'd acted like he didn't care because it was easier. Safer. He'd convinced himself he didn't care, but he knew then, with that fury beating through his blood, that he did. About a lot of the things—the hotel, the town, his dysfunctional family, Meghan. He didn't know if he could make any of it come right but he wanted to try. He chose to fight.

He closed his eyes, breathing in the fresh scent that now permeated the place and let the memories come. For so many years his early childhood had been nothing but a blank, but now he wanted to open that door his subconscious had swung shut so long ago. He wanted to remember everything—the awful as well as the good. The grief as well as the joy.

Now, his eyes closed, he pictured his father bringing in

the Christmas tree. Felt his hand on his head. Heard the laughter. Saw his brothers, standing by the stairs, smiling and joking. And he knew that whatever was between them now, they'd once been a real family. A happy family.

And maybe they could be again.

As for him and Meghan… he was still afraid of letting her down. If he didn't get Adam to agree to keep the hotel, would she see him as a failure and walk away from him? It felt as if everything was on the line.

He had everything to fight for… and he wanted to win.

MEGHAN SPENT A restless night wondering what Quinn was doing and thinking, and wishing he was with her. She'd gotten used to sleeping in his arms, having him firmly in her life. And she realized, as she stared gritty-eyed at the ceiling, the dawn light filtering through the curtains of her bedroom, that hotel or not, she wanted Quinn in her life. They could both change, grow. Together.

As soon as Betty had picked up Polly for work, Meghan headed over to the hotel. She breathed a sigh of relief when she saw the truck in the parking lot. She'd been half-afraid he might have left in the night.

"Hello?" she called as she opened the door to the kitchen. "Anybody home?"

"In here." She followed Quinn's voice to the dining room, where he was sitting on the bare floor, a notebook on his knees.

"What are you doing?"

"Just writing some stuff down." He glanced up at her with a smile; Meghan thought he looked tired. "For Adam."

"You're going to talk to him?"

"Yeah, I'm going to drive down there today." He let out a little laugh. "Considering I just phoned the real estate agent and canceled the listing, I'd better get a move on. Adam's going to blow a gasket when he finds out."

"What are you going to say to him?"

"I'm going to remind him of a few things." Quinn tossed the notebook and stood up. "I don't know if it will work—"

"It doesn't matter if it works," Meghan blurted. Quinn stared at her in surprise. "I mean, it matters. Of course it does. But I wanted to tell you that it doesn't matter to me. To us. I… I love you, Quinn." Meghan felt heat surge into her face. She hadn't actually planned on using the L-word quite so soon.

"That's good, because I love you too." Quinn strode toward her and pulled her into his arms. "I wanted to tell you first."

"Beat you to it, I guess," she mumbled and buried her head in his chest.

"Hey… hey." Quinn stroked her hair, his arms still around her. "What's this? You're not crying, are you?"

"Not exactly," Meghan said, sniffing. "I just feel emotional. I didn't even know if you'd be here this morning."

"Where else would I be?"

"I thought you might have decided you'd had enough of all of us. Of me—"

"Hey, how about some confidence? I don't scare that easily."

"I know, but…" Meghan's voice wobbled. "Everyone else did."

Quinn frowned. "What do you mean?"

"My mom, my dad. Ben. It was a long time ago, but they all left. I guess that's what I've gotten used to."

"That's understandable," Quinn said as he gently tilted her chin up so she could meet his gaze. "But I'm not leaving, Meghan. I'm going to New York today and I'll be back tomorrow, I promise. And then you'll have a whole lot of trouble getting rid of me."

"What if Adam says no?"

"I don't know," Quinn admitted. "But whatever happens with the hotel or the town, I still want to be with you."

Her heart felt as if it were expanding, a balloon of hope and lightness filling her chest. "And I still want to be with you."

Quinn pulled her back into his arms for a tight, fierce hug. "Good," he said. "Then that's settled, at least."

FIVE HOURS LATER Quinn sat across from his mother in the large formal drawing room of the Freemans' townhouse on Fifth Avenue.

"I thought you'd left yesterday," Margo had said when

Dorothy had ushered him into the room. She'd stood up and offered her cheek for him to kiss.

"I did leave," Quinn said. "And I came back." He took a deep breath, wanting to shield his mother from pain but knowing what needed to be said. "I'm going to ask Adam not to sell the hotel, Mom. I want to keep it in the family. I want to open it again."

Margo flinched as if Quinn had struck her, her face paling. "Quinn…"

"Are you really against the idea?" Quinn asked quietly. "I know you don't like to talk about the hotel or Creighton Falls, but you're the one who asked me to go up there and have a look." He studied her face, looking for some acknowledgement in her eyes that he was on the right track and not just guessing wildly. "I think at least part of you wanted me to bring that place back to life and not just get rid of it." Quinn saw the conflict in his mother's face but she didn't speak. "If you just wanted to get rid of the place, you would have had Adam sell it. Why involve me?"

"I knew you never had any memories," Margo said after a long pause. "I thought maybe… maybe it would help."

"So you wanted me to remember?"

"I don't know." She let out a shaky laugh. "I've spent twenty-two years trying not to remember, Quinn. I know that makes me a coward. The happiest years of my life were in Creighton Falls and I act like I want to forget them all." She sighed and bit her lip. "If I were a stronger woman, I would have kept those memories alive for you boys. But it was so very difficult... you could never know how much. How broken I was. Only Adam..." She drew a deep breath. "Adam saw me at my worst, which is why he's so protective of me. Why he never wants to mention Creighton Falls."

"And you?" Quinn asked. "Why have you never wanted to remember?"

"Because it was too painful. Not just for me, but for Adam and Jake. You didn't remember, but they... they had it hard, Quinn. They saw things..."

"What kind of things?"

Margo's voice trembled. "I wasn't a good mother back then, Quinn. I wasn't a whole person. And I wanted to escape, and then once I did it felt like there was no going back. And maybe there isn't." She glanced up at him, her eyes full of both tears and doubt.

"You can't go back," Quinn agreed slowly, "but you can go forward. We can make the hotel something good again, for us and for the town. Maybe if we do that, the past won't have such a hold on us anymore. Because it does, doesn't it?" He reached for her hands. "I couldn't remember a thing about the first six years of my life, but I was still hostage to it," he said, remembering Meghan's words. "To the guilt—"

Margo's eyes widened. "Why should you feel guilty—"

"Because Dad died trying to save me." The stark words made Margo flinch again.

"It was an accident, Quinn. No one ever blamed you—"

Quinn let out a harsh laugh. "I'm not so sure about that, Mom."

"You don't think I—"

"No," he said after a moment. "But Adam—and Jake—"

"No. No. I hate to think that." She shook her head, her hands pressed to her face.

Quinn stared at her. "Why did we never talk about it, then? Not once that I can remember. What kind of family doesn't remember the father they all loved?" His voice rang out harshly and he realized, to his own shock, that he was angry. His mother had always been someone to shelter and protect, to keep from experiencing even more of life's sorrows. But now, for the first time, Quinn realized how his mother had let them all down. How she'd let her own grief trump theirs. "We should have talked about him," he said, and his mother let out a choked sob, tears trickling down her face.

"Oh Quinn, Quinn. I'm sorry." Margo hid her face in her hands and with guilt rushing through him like acid, Quinn moved to embrace her.

"I'm sorry, Mom. I didn't mean to make you cry."

"But you're right," she said, her voice muffled through her fingers. "You're right. I've been so selfish. It was just I couldn't bear… and your brothers didn't want to talk about it, either." She glanced up at him, her face wet with tears. "And you didn't either, but I didn't realize it was because you blamed yourself. Oh, Quinn—"

"It doesn't matter now," he said, sitting back in his chair. "We've been hostage to the past enough. It's time to think of the future. The future of our family, and the future of the hotel."

Margo drew a shuddering breath. "Do you really want to open it?"

"Yes." As he said it he realized how true it was. He wanted this. For himself, for Meghan, for all of Creighton Falls. "Yes, Mom, I want to open the hotel. I want to help run it. I want Jake and Adam to help too. It was our home once—"

"I know, Quinn." Her mother gave him a wan smile. "And I think it's what your father would have wanted. He loved that place. It always hurt to think of how it had gone to ruin."

And yet you still did nothing. Quinn kept himself from saying the words. He didn't blame his mother for giving into grief. He'd given into guilt. But no longer.

"Adam's going to resist," he said flatly. "He always does. Seven years ago it was my thirty percent against your seventy—"

"Oh, Quinn." Margo shook her head. "Is that what you thought?"

"What was I supposed to think? You all voted against me."

"I was trying to free you," Margo said. "I didn't want you to be saddled with the company's burdens when you were so young—"

"Even though I'd asked to be?"

"You were young," Margo insisted. "You didn't know what you were taking on."

There might have been some truth to that, but Quinn didn't want to argue the point. He wanted to look toward the future. "The point is," he said, "this time the vote needs to go the other way."

TWENTY MINUTES LATER Quinn was standing in the waiting area outside Adam's penthouse office in midtown.

"Mr. Freeman will see you now," the receptionist said primly, and Quinn took a steadying breath. He wasn't going to pick a fight with his brother. Not this time.

"You sent the real estate agent packing," Adam said as soon as Quinn had opened the door. "Not funny, Quinn."

Quinn closed the door behind him. "It wasn't meant to be funny."

"What the hell do you think you're playing at?"

"I'm not playing. I don't want to sell the hotel—"

"That doesn't matter."

"As pleasant as usual, I see," Quinn said before he could keep himself from it. "What the hell is wrong with you, Adam?" Adam blinked at him, shocked, and Quinn took a step forward. "I know we haven't seen eye to eye on basically anything, but you'll hear me out on this. The hotel deserves a second chance. I spoke to Mom and she's agreed to keep it open."

"You spoke to *Mom* about this?"

"Yes."

Color surged into Adam's face. "Damn it, Quinn, hasn't she suffered enough?"

"Haven't we all?" Quinn challenged. "It's time to create something good out of what happened, Adam. We can't run away forever."

"As far as I can see, you're the only one who has been running away."

"We have different ways of doing the same thing."

"Cute, but no thanks—"

"I'm not asking your permission," Quinn returned. "I own thirty percent of the company shares, as you know. And this time I'm not going to let you manipulate everyone to vote against me."

"You're still angry about that? You were twenty years old, Quinn, with a GPA that was in the basement—"

"I was your brother, and Dad wanted us all involved, which is why he divided the shares equally. You could have given me a chance."

"I couldn't risk it." Adam's expression darkened and closed. "You have no idea how seriously I take my responsibility. How I have to."

"Then tell me, Adam. Tell me what's driving you. What makes you claw back control like the world is going to spin off its axis if you're not in charge."

Adam rubbed a hand over his face. "You wouldn't understand."

"You could try me," Quinn answered. "Why do you think I want to reopen the hotel? Not just to help a town, but to help, to heal, our *family*. We're not happy, are we, Adam, as a family? You're not happy."

Adam's eyes glittered as he lifted his chin. "It doesn't matter if I'm happy or not."

"Don't you think Dad would want you to be happy? Reopening the hotel would do something else." Quinn took a deep breath. "It would honor Dad."

Adam flinched, his face contorting before his features smoothed out to iron blandness. He didn't speak.

"I remember him, Adam," Quinn said softly. "I didn't before. I didn't remember a thing about him or anything before I was six. But since coming back to Creighton Falls I've started remembering, and I *like* what I remember." A muscle flickered in Adam's temple but he still said nothing. Quinn continued, his voice choking a little, "I remember Dad cutting down our Christmas tree. I remember him laughing with me, and telling stupid knock-knock jokes, and wrestling with all three of us." The words were coming faster now, the memories running like a blurry film reel through his mind. "I remember him joking about doing the Jimmy Snuka Superfly. I remember he smelled like the peppermints he always ate. I *remember.*" The last word was spoken on a gasp.

Adam's expression didn't change. He didn't speak, and

Quinn stared at him, despair sweeping through him. He wasn't going to be able to convince him, and if Adam turned it into a battle, there would be nothing he could do. Sixty percent would prevail.

"Fine," Adam said at last. Quinn blinked at him in surprise. "Take the hotel. Do what you want with it. But don't involve me."

"But... you'd have to be involved, Adam. In some way—"

"No." Adam's voice was flat, final. "I'll set up a separate bank account for the place. You can access the old files and accounts. But I don't want to know anything about it."

This was victory, but it felt bittersweet. "Adam..."

"Be satisfied with that, Quinn," Adam said as he turned away to stare out the window, his hands jammed in the pockets of his trousers. "You can't turn us back into the family we once were. I can't be that innocent kid anymore. But you can have your damn hotel."

Looking at Adam's tense profile, Quinn felt a surprising flicker of sympathy for his oldest brother. He might not have remembered anything about Creighton Falls and his father's accident, but Adam clearly did.

"Thank you, Adam," he said and his brother jerked his head in the semblance of a nod.

IT WAS A crazy thing to do, but Meghan felt a little crazy. She'd enlisted the help of Billy Kargas, Brenda Wickley, Hannah and Sam Taylor, and Beth Lindell, the woman who had recently bought the general store. She needed all of their help to get the sign positioned right, across the porch of the hotel.

Billy scratched his head as he looked at the banner flapping in the brisk spring breeze. "But what if he doesn't reopen the hotel?"

"It doesn't matter," Meghan said firmly. "He's still coming back, and this is still his home."

"So who are these Freemans, exactly?" Beth asked.

Meghan laughed. "You've been here nearly a week and you haven't heard of the Freemans? Do I have a lot to tell you."

"I'll fill her in," Hannah promised. "Especially about Quinn."

"Hannah." Shaking her head, Meghan slipped her cellphone out of her pocket, as she'd been doing about twenty times an hour since Quinn left. No messages. Reception was patchy and sometimes texts or voicemails didn't come through for hours. Quinn might have tried to get in touch. But maybe he hadn't. Even now she felt a flicker of uncertainty, a tremor of fear. She had no idea what Quinn was experiencing in New York, or if it would change his feelings about Creighton Falls. About her.

Hannah laid a hand on her arm. "It's going to be okay, Meghan."

"Am I that obvious?"

"Pretty much, but so is Quinn, and that man is crazy

about you."

"I'm crazy about him." Meghan closed her eyes briefly. "I haven't felt this way about anybody before, Han. It's scary, to feel so much."

"I know. But it's good too, right? It's really living."

"Yeah." Meghan managed a wobbly smile. She really wanted to hear from Quinn. "I should go pick up Polly."

"I heard she went to a Bucks game with your dad," Hannah said, her eyebrows raised. "That's new."

"Yeah." Meghan shook her head, still smiling. "But good. My dad's going to get more involved, I think."

"It's about time."

"I think he wanted to for a while. I was the one holding him back, even though I didn't realize it."

"Understandable," Hannah murmured. "No one wants to set themselves up for disappointment."

"Right." And she hoped she wasn't setting herself up for disappointment now. He'd call soon, she told herself. He'd let her know what had happened, and he'd reassure her that he still loved her.

QUINN TOSSED HIS phone onto the passenger seat of his Beamer as he pulled out of the rest stop on Highway 81. Less than hour until he got back to Creighton Falls. He'd talked to Jake for over an hour on the phone, and asked his brother's help with the hotel.

"Consider this your next rescue project," he'd told Jake.

"A whole town needs your help to recover from a different kind of disaster."

Jake hadn't been sure at first. "I don't know, Quinn. Creighton Falls…"

"Needs your help. Seriously, Jake. Reopening the hotel isn't going to be the magic fix everyone thinks it will be. It's a start, but the town needs a lot of work to turn it back into a tourist destination."

"It's not quite the same as recovering bodies from a plane crash," Jake said dryly.

"There are some surprising similarities. And we owe this town, Jake, whether you think that or not. I know it's true. I've been there. We all walked away without a backward glance and it's time we came back."

Jake sighed. "I've got a couple of weeks free. I'll come up next weekend and have a look. But I'm not promising anything."

"Of course not."

Now Quinn tapped his fingers against the steering wheel, eager to be back in Creighton Falls, with Meghan in his arms. He'd tried texting her but the reception had been bad and then his phone had gone dead, and he'd forgotten to bring the charging cord. But he'd see her soon enough, and he'd tell her everything then.

He drove slowly through the town, savoring the view of the pine trees by the side of the road, the sweeping porches on the Victorian houses, even the glint of the river, sparkling under a setting sun. He'd broken a few speeding limits trying to get here as fast as he could. He hoped Meghan was at home.

He slowed as he came to the green, and he saw the crowd outside the hotel. Worry lurched inside him—what had gone wrong? Was someone hurt? He saw Brenda Wickley, Billy Kargas, the Taylors, and a bunch of other people he knew by sight. He pulled in front of the hotel, about to roll down his window and ask what was wrong, when he saw the sign.

Welcome Home Quinn.

He saw Meghan in the center of the crowd, smiling, all her hope and love in her eyes, and Quinn felt tears sting his own. No one knew that he'd saved the hotel, but they were welcoming him home anyway. Accepting him, loving him in a way he'd never felt before. He wasn't the screw-up here. He wasn't the disappointment.

Smiling, he got out of the car.

Meghan walked toward him, her arms outstretched, Polly right behind her, dancing on her tiptoes. "I missed you," Meghan said, and Quinn pulled her into a tight embrace.

"You're amazing."

"*You're* amazing—"

"Is this a contest?" he murmured against her hair. "You don't even know what's happened with the hotel."

"I told you I don't care about that, Quinn."

"I believe you." He took a deep breath, his heart so wonderfully full. "But I hope you care enough to order a whole lot of copper piping. No more patch jobs for The Creighton Falls Hotel."

She pulled back, her eyes wide as she searched his face. "Seriously?"

"Seriously."

She launched herself at him then, wrapping arms and legs around him as she buried her face in his neck, and Polly got in on the hug too. Laughing, Quinn put one arm around Meghan and another around Polly.

"I knew you could do it," Meghan said fiercely.

Around him people were laughing and cheering, and Billy Kargas clapped him so hard on the back he nearly staggered.

"Only with your help," Quinn told Meghan, and then he kissed her.

"Ew," Polly exclaimed, and everyone cheered harder. Quinn looked around at all the people he'd come to know as friends and smiled. "We're going to need a *lot* of help," he told them, and then he kissed Meghan again.

LATER, LYING ON Meghan's sofa, their legs tangled together and Meghan's head resting on Quinn's chest, they talked more about the hotel.

"Do you really want this?" Meghan asked. "I'm worried I pushed you into it."

Quinn toyed with a strand of Meghan's hair. "You worry

too much."

"Maybe I do. Maybe I need to let go a little bit more. A *lot* more."

He dropped his hand to the dip of her waist, his fingers inching higher. "I think I can help you with that."

"*Quinn,*" Meghan protested, but she didn't push his hand away. "As long as you're happy."

"I'm one hundred percent happy, Meghan. With the hotel, with Creighton Falls, with you."

"And Polly…"

"And Polly," he affirmed. "I love Polly, Meghan. She's part of my life just as she's part of yours." He tilted her chin so she met his gaze. "I've traveled the world and there's nowhere else I'd rather be right now—and forever."

She turned her head so her lips brushed his fingers. "That means so much to me, Quinn. I'm sorry that I have trouble believing that sometimes. It's my issue, not yours."

"You can plan on me sticking around to help you sort out your issues," Quinn promised. He brought her hand to his lips, nibbling the tips of her fingers. "But I think there's a significant issue we need to work on right now…"

Laughing, Meghan wriggled her way under him. "I think you're absolutely right," she said, and then she reached up and kissed him.

THE END

Introducing Kate Hewitt's new series…

FALLING FOR THE FREEMANS

Find out what happens when the Freeman brothers return to Creighton Falls.

Falling for Christmas
Book 1: Sam and Hannah's story

Falling Hard
Book 2: Quinn and Meghan's story

Falling Fast
Book 3: Jake and Beth's story

ABOUT THE AUTHOR

After spending three years as a diehard New Yorker,
Katharine Swartz now lives in the Lake District in England with
her husband, their five children, and a Golden Retriever. She
enjoys such novel things as long country walks and chatting with
people in the street, and her children love the freedom of village
life—although she often has to ring four or five people to figure
out where they've gone off to.

She writes women's fiction as well as contemporary romance
under the name Kate Hewitt, and whatever the genre she enjoys
delivering a compelling and intensely emotional story.

You can find out more about Katharine on her website at
kate-hewitt.com

Thank you for reading

FALLING HARD

If you enjoyed this book, you can find more from all our great authors at TulePublishing.com, or from your favorite online retailer.

TULE
PUBLISHING

Printed in Great Britain
by Amazon